'You know, I don't think that it has ever been better than that,' he told her.

Sandra nodded happily. 'Don't laugh at me, but I feel as if there has been a new sort of magic ever since we've had that odd bit of metal in the room.'

'That's no way to refer to the solid gold penis of a god,' Donald grinned. 'But I know what you mean: it does make you feel that it exercises an eerie kind of influence.'

There certainly was a mysterious aura about the strange object which was destined to exert so powerful an attraction over so many people in the coming months . . .

By the same author

*The Happy Hooker*
*Letters to the Happy Hooker*
*Xaviera!*
*The Best Part of a Man*
*Xaviera's Supersex*
*Xaviera Goes Wild!*
*Xaviera Meets Marilyn Chambers*
   (with Marilyn Chambers)
*Knights in the Garden of Spain*
*Xaviera's Magic Mushrooms*
*Madame l'Ambassadrice*
*The Inner Circle*
*Lucinda, My Lovely*
*Fiesta of the Flesh*
*Lucinda, Hot Nights on Xanthos*
*Happily Hooked* (with John Drummond)
*Erotic Enterprises Inc.*
*Yours Fatally!*
*Prisoner of the Firebird*

# XAVIERA HOLLANDER

# The Kiss of the Serpent

Book Two of the
*Golden Phallus of Osiris* trilogy

This edition published 1995
by Diamond Books
77–85 Fulham Palace Road
Hammersmith, London W6 8JB

First published by Grafton Books 1987

ISBN 0 261 66647 9

Printed and bound in Great Britain

Set in Times

# Contents

# Part I

# 1

## The Serpent of Old Nile

As the boat ran on to the white sands of the beach, the only sound to greet them was the incessant crashing of the breakers on the shore. Standing, waiting for them in absolute silence, were two men, tall, dark-skinned, grim-faced. The three passengers scrambled out of the proa, and waded through the surf. The stars were dazzlingly brilliant and the light of the moon was sufficient for them to be able to see clearly their surroundings, the jagged cliffs and the lush vegetation beyond.

Without saying a word, the two sentinels turned and led them past the line of giant palm trees which fringed the beach, to where a steep path led through the tropical forest. They were a strangely incongruous group, following the track on this tiny, uncharted island, not far over the horizon from Bali. The woman, Cleo Janis, a vivacious blonde in her late thirties, lived in Los Angeles, where she was quite a celebrity in the entertainment business, managing a stable of stars and organizing pop concerts and festivals all over the world. Beside her strode Andrew Drummond, a Scottish-born doctor with a thriving and fashionable practice in London. A gaunt, athletic man in his mid-fifties, with his iron-grey hair and cold blue eyes behind heavy tortoise-shell-rimmed glasses, he maintained an air of distinction, despite the informal clothes he was wearing. Behind him panted a tubby, bald-headed man of much the same age, but in much worse condition. Josef Grunwald was a director of one of the largest banks in Zurich, and a lifetime behind his massive desk had done nothing to confine the spread of his wandering waistline.

After they had been climbing for ten minutes, the pitch-black mouth of a large cavern opened up on their left, and the two silent guides led the party inside. They had to grope in the dark for a few paces, and then the path turned a corner, and their way was lit by flickering torches lining the rock walls. Their footsteps echoed as they followed the corridor which ended at a smooth face of grey stone. However, at their approach, a part of the apparently solid rock swung back, and the wall was transformed into a door, through which they filed. The visitors gave a gasp of wonder at the scene before their eyes.

Carved into the living rock was a replica of an ancient Egyptian temple, its colonnade of great round columns brilliantly decorated with painted hieroglyphics. Two huge statues faced them, one of a human figure with the head of a dog.

'My God, that's Anubis!' exclaimed Andrew Drummond.

One of the escorts wheeled round. 'Silence! You have been warned. Do not utter one more word until the priestess, Isis, has spoken.'

The three strangers gazed around them. The temple was dimly lit by lamps of coloured glass, which resembled those of a later period to be found in the mosques of Baghdad or Damascus, but which blended well with the mysterious cave. Near the walls, there were stone benches, and ledges on which stood various strange objects – a gold and topaz amulet, a curiously wrought sceptre, and the gorgeously illustrated papyrus manuscript of the Egyptian *Book of the Dead*. At the back of this pagan shrine was a door, presumably leading to an inner chamber, from which there emerged eight figures, dressed in the simple linen robes of priests, each wearing a different ornate head-dress. They took up their positions before the other statue, a solemn, larger-than-life wooden carving of the goddess Isis, the double crown of Upper and Lower Egypt upon her head, a royal whip in one hand and a ruby, deep, brooding, red and large as a pigeon's egg, carved into the form of a scarab, at her breast.

Only when the front of the statue began to move did they realize that what they were looking at was in fact a mummy case, and that it was not empty. Slowly, the door pivoted on its hinges, and from inside there stepped a woman, dressed precisely the same as the statue of Isis in which she had been entombed. She was tall and slender and magnificent: her glossy black hair and brilliant almond-shaped eyes, darkened by kohl, made her as superb as if she were indeed the goddess herself. Her appearance was dramatically beautiful, for not only was she endowed with the stateliness of one who was born to be obeyed but, more than that, she was the essence of all the sexuality of the world made living flesh and blood. No man or woman could look at such perfection without falling instantly beneath her spell. The eight priests sank to their knees before her. The escorts nudged the visitors and they too knelt.

'Behold the priestess of Isis,' intoned one of the priests.

There was a long silence and then Isis began to speak. Her voice was deep and husky, but she chanted her words, as if she were reading some ancient incantation which cast a spell over her listeners.

'Strangers, know that the powers of the great goddess, Isis, reside in me. I am her priestess, but when I speak, I become the goddess herself. Know me as Isis. No man can resist my will and my servants, scattered throughout the world, worship and obey the goddess who has come

11

back from the Land of the Shades to live again in my body. And you have been chosen to serve also. You will be shown the secrets of sexual domination which will compel all men and women to adore you and to obey you, just as you must be subject to me.

'Before the ritual of initiation, know this. The great god, Osiris, consort of Isis, was trapped by Seth, the Evil One, who killed him and cut My Lord's body into thirteen parts, which he then buried in every corner of the earth. But such was the power of love that Isis wandered through every land, until she had recovered each severed limb, the flesh and bones of divine Osiris. With needle and thread, she restored the body, and with her lips she pressed on his the kiss of life. Then, when Osiris was once more master of the Twin Kingdoms of Egypt, their son, the mighty Horus, sought out and slew Seth. Yet Osiris was not whole, nor could he ever again enjoy Isis, for one part of his body remained always hidden, buried deep in the earth. Neither Isis nor any other seeker has been able to find the phallus of Osiris. But, even though it remains in the womb of the earth, so potent is it that it never ceases to impregnate the fruitful earth which therefore brings forth its rich harvest, year in and year out.

'This legend is known to you, as it is to all mankind. But we who serve Isis know something more. During the time when the body of Osiris was scattered, a great golden statue, resembling his body in every particular, was made. It, too, in a symbolic ceremony, was divided into thirteen parts which also were buried. By consulting the necromantic potency of this statue, the goddess was able to divine the whereabouts of the body of her beloved. We, her followers, have vowed to seek out those hidden parts of the golden statue and to rebuild it, as a shrine to the goddess, and to the magical powers of carnal love. You, who are about to join with us in this cult of libido, in the service of Isis, will also dedicate yourselves to the same quest. Follow me.'

Isis turned and walked into the inner chamber, followed by her attendants, who flanked the three postulants. They found themselves in a small circular room, the walls of which were panelled in scarlet velvet. Tall candles, in golden sconces, cast sinister shadows, and the air was charged by some exotic aroma which aroused in them a subtle excitement, as though something fantastic was about to happen to them. Before them were drawn up three oriental divans, their wooden backs decorated with carvings of Egyptian hawk-headed deities and coiling serpents. Cleo Janis was motioned to be seated on the first, and her companions were placed on those on either side of her. Isis stood before them, and began to read from a papyrus scroll, as ancient as the very pharaohs.

None of them could ever explain subsequently what happened next. The voice of Isis seeped into their brains, dulling their senses, but quickening their emotions. They remembered not one word of that insidious chant.

Cleo gazed at Isis, and everybody else faded into oblivion. The priestess glided towards her, until Cleo could savour the fragrant scent of her breath. Her skin was as smooth as porcelain, flawless, ivory-hued, and as delicate as a rose petal. Cleo's hands stretched forward, as if of their own volition, and as she touched the warm flesh, a tingling ran through her body. The face of Isis showed no trace of feeling, and her lips continued to mouth those strange words in an unknown language. But Cleo experienced a surge of lust, utterly different from, and vastly stronger than, anything she had ever known. Every fibre of her body ached to be part of the gorgeous woman who was now so close to her. She had no recollection of either of them taking off their clothes, but she found herself naked, and feasting her eyes on the nude figure of the priestess. Never had she seen a body so immaculately formed, and it was with reverence that she took her in her arms. Their lips touched, and Isis passively accepted her embrace. Cleo's hands roamed over her body, fondling her firm, small breasts, stroking the slender waist and the voluptuous swell of her hips. Yet, even when Cleo had buried her head in Isis's crotch, and tasted the nectar which flowed from the lips of her vagina, the priestess remained aloof and unresponsive, but her very indifference inspired Cleo to even more demonstrative passion. She dropped to the ground and covered Isis's feet with kisses. And although this goddess of sensuality did not condescend to touch her, Cleo felt the throbbing of her own soaking cunt, the tautening of her nipples, and the wild hurricane of her orgasm tore through her consciousness, so that she feared that she would lose her reason. With her eyes closed, she fought for breath, her body possessed by this sublime being from another world and another age.

But when the fury had passed, and she was lying, limp and prostrate, Cleo opened her eyes to find that she was still on her couch, fully dressed, and Isis was continuing to read from the papyrus, far away from her. Only the wetness of her panties remained as a reminder of that brief, glorious encounter.

Andrew Drummond knew nothing of the sweetness which had transfigured Cleo. He listened to the intoning of Isis, and without any conscious effort on his part, he understood. She was telling him that Time was not a great ocean, but a tiny puddle, over which he could stride effortlessly. And so he stepped across the abyss of the Past. She was still there, in front of him, Isis in all her divine splendour, but he had become Osiris. Seth was dead, and he was triumphant, a king about to take his queen. His body was that of an eternally young god, glowing and potent. Isis pointed in wonder at his penis, long, rigid, rampant.

'My Lord,' she breathed. 'See, you are complete and unblemished. Surely it is my love that has made you whole.'

He clasped her, and he felt her body yielding to his. He was strong, proud in his manhood. He knew that his destiny demanded that he penetrate Isis and impregnate her, that she might be fertile as the Nile. He, and only he, could quicken life within her womb. So he took her, and she submitted to him. And what bliss it was, as he inhaled her subtly female odour, while the soft, moist warmth of her drew him into those mysterious depths of her body. While they made love, the very earth danced for sheer joy. As they moved, faster and faster, in that perfect rhythm which can only be attained when two people have become completely one, her limbs were his, and at the same time, she possessed all of him. He did not feel ecstasy: he created it! With every thrust, he was the Lion, the lord of Africa, and she was the Serpent, the mistress of wisdom and witchcraft. But together, they were the divine lust which ruled the world. The stars were spinning around them, and the moon burst into a thousand fragments at the moment that he pumped into her the precious seed which she seemed to suck in eagerly with each contraction of her wildly pulsating vagina.

An eternity passed, and Andrew Drummond was once more back on his divan, gazing rapturously at the solemnly apparelled figure before him, still holding her papyrus scroll. Had it been a vision, or had he, for a fleeting moment, been part of something too deep for him to comprehend? One thing was certain: his ejaculation had been real enough, a veritable flood.

And what of Josef Grunwald? Reclining on his divan, he too had known the goddess, in his own fashion. Her voice was boring into his brain, filling him with a strange numbness, and dissolving all the conventional restraints which had governed the regular, unchanging routine which had been his life. His hand stroked the wooden serpent at the back of the divan, and he felt it grow warm and begin to stir beneath his touch. But his eyes were fixed on the nubile figure before him. How could it be that, while his fingers caressed a wooden carving, what he felt was the satin-soft skin of the priestess? He was feverish: he could hear the blood pulsing through his veins and his breathing was becoming ragged. But all these strange sensations were dominated by an overwhelming compulsion to abase himself before the supernatural loveliness of Isis.

She was still standing erect, arrogant, cold and unapproachable. Josef threw himself at her feet, silently imploring her to receive his adoration, and show him some slight acknowledgement of his existence. His penis had swollen to a fierce tumescence which ached unbearably. If only she were to have pity on him in some way, he would be able to find relief. Raising his eyes, he found that Isis had turned her back on him, and shrugged off her white robe. He climbed to his knees, and gratefully embraced the globes of her tight buttocks. As if in answer to his wordless prayer, Isis parted her legs and offered her arse to his thirsting lips. She tasted salt and tangy, but to his tongue, this was pure nectar. As his grip on her thighs tightened, he could feel his erection growing more and more insistent. All his being was centred in that huge, tormented member which was laid as a tribute to the goddess at her feet.

Did it last a mere moment or was there an eternity which passed before he gave voice to a despairing scream, and a spurt of thick, white sperm gushed forth, and he fell back, exhausted and annihilated? Time had no meaning until Josef went to rise from the dusty ground, and discovered that he was already on the divan, and the white-robed priestess was still reading aloud from the papyrus, as remote as the silver moon. Had it all been a hallucination and this weird, and as it now seemed to him rather sordid, sexual experience had never physically occurred? The cold, sticky wetness in his pants convinced him that something had taken place, and that despite all her apparent lack of concern, Isis had witnessed and accepted his gesture of submission. In this knowledge, he found a glow of contentment.

At last, it came to an end. Isis reverently rolled up the scroll, which was taken from her by one of her attendants. There was no sudden breaking of the spell; instead, a gradual easing of the tension, like the slow melting away of a morning mist. The three stirred on their couches, and began to look around them as though they had just awakened. Isis spoke to them again.

'Remember what has happened to you, and know that this power to inspire divine lust is the gift of the goddess. Now that you are her servants, it will be shared with you, so that you can play your parts in bringing nearer the day when the whole world will acknowledge the rule of Isis and Osiris. But that will not come about until the body of the Lord Osiris is restored once more, not in the mortal flesh which has perished long ago, but in the great golden statue. Let your eyes be witness.'

Isis turned away and walked to a niche in the rock wall from which two of her escorts, broad-shouldered, muscular men, lifted with a great effort something long and obviously very heavy which they carried to the row of divans. The three visitors stared in astonishment at a perfectly formed arm and hand of solid gold. The fingers

17

had been worked with minute care, the achievement of a master craftsman.

'Gee,' Cleo breathed incredulously, 'the folks back in Hollywood would give an arm and a leg for that arm and hand!'

'Please, it is permitted for me to examine, yes?' Josef Grunwald was clearly impressed by the object. 'My bank handles more bullion than any other financial institution. Should your organization be interested at any time in disposing, feel at liberty to contact me. I shall give you my business card.'

'Silence!' thundered Isis. 'We have brought this fragment of the statue here as proof for you that somewhere the remainder of the god's body is waiting for those of us who serve Isis. We already have, in various sanctuaries, most of the body, but still we seek. If we discover the most deeply hidden of all, the Golden Phallus, and the statue were then to be reborn, we would be endowed with powers of which, in your state of ignorance, you can have no conception. Now you must depart from this place, but each of you will be summoned by me, or you must invoke me, should the need arise.'

The silent sentinels led them back along the path to the shore, where the proa was waiting for them, its triangular sail flapping idly in the faint breeze. They climbed aboard, and the flimsy craft was pushed off the beach. Soon the tiny island was lost to sight in the early morning mist. Nobody spoke. One question was in the mind of each of them. How long would they have to wait before the summons would come, the command to undertake an unknown task in the service of Isis? Meanwhile, they would return to their normal lives and wait.

# 2

## *Bear with a Sore Head*

Asi Moriba skipped nimbly in front of the blue and cream tramcar as he crossed the Paradeplatz. He had always admired the view here, in the heart of Zurich, with imposing buildings on each side, all of them housing some of the most important banks in the world. He used to declare that it gave him a sense of security to be surrounded by all that money. The fact that quite a sizeable amount of it belonged to him was even more reassuring.

He was an enormous man, and he walked with the swagger of somebody accustomed to the ruthless use of absolute power. Moriba had been appointed the boss of the police forces of the African state of Salamba when it achieved independence, and in a very short time he had become the most feared man in the country. When the president of Salamba had been assassinated, Moriba had seized power, but had been forced to flee, following an uprising which had overthrown the regime. Now his hated rival, the anarchist Milos, who had for years been hunted by Moriba, had replaced him.

But Moriba was resilient and resourceful, and in one of those financial cathedrals, overlooking the Paradeplatz, there was waiting for him the hoard which he had accumulated during the years when he had virtually run Salamba and unashamedly skimmed off astronomical sums from the exploitation of the great mineral wealth of the country.

He pushed open the armoured glass door and strode through the spacious banking hall. Ignoring the people standing at the counters, Moriba summoned one of the managers who chanced to be walking by, and demanded to see the director of the bank who personally looked after his affairs. The black giant was not the sort of man, once seen, who could easily be forgotten, and he was immediately ushered into a discreet waiting-room.

Josef Grunwald was presiding over a meeting of the bank's investment committee when he was informed of Moriba's arrival. He hastily handed over the conduct of the meeting to one of his assistants, and scuttled out of the room. He ordered the statements of Moriba's accounts and security portfolio to be brought to the waiting-room, and then joined his visitor.

'My dear Moriba, I cannot tell you how sorry I was to hear of the unfortunate events in Salamba. How on earth did you manage to get away?'

Grunwald's expression was that of an undertaker conveying professional condolences, but Moriba was in a hearty mood, and laughed off his fussy sympathy.

'How does one always get out of a crisis?' He chuckled. 'I lied, robbed, cheated and murdered. It was just like any other day when I was running the secret police.'

'You have always had such a strong sense of humour,' Grunwald replied uncertainly. 'But are you safe, or will they chase you in Europe?'

'Milos will have enough on his hands without bothering to come after me, as long as I leave him in peace. I know the man. He has got what he wanted, and he has no interest in whatever I might get up to outside Salamba.' Moriba spoke with easy confidence.

'And now, do you have any plans?' enquired Grunwald nervously.

'Plenty,' answered Moriba, with a wide grin. 'But they will need money.' For half an hour the two men examined the bank statements and Moriba made arrangements to withdraw cash for his immediate requirements.

'So, now where are you going? Or do you intend to stay in Zurich for a while?'

'Zurich isn't my kind of city,' Moriba told him. 'It's too correct and proper – a clinical sort of place. I need somewhere very different. I was thinking of Rome.'

'Rome is very pleasant, a wonderful cultural centre,' Grunwald assented.

'Culture!' snorted Moriba derisively. 'It is absolutely corrupt, one racket after another, and full of whores, pimps and pushers. In fact, just like Salamba. Think of the opportunities it offers a man with my talents and experience!'

Grunwald smiled weakly. He had always been afraid of this great bull of a man, and he would dearly have liked to cut short the interview, but the prospect of offending Moriba terrified him. So he assured Moriba that, once he was established in Rome, Grunwald would give the necessary instructions for him to be able to draw money from a local bank.

'Well, you seem in surprisingly good spirits,' commented the banker. 'Don't you regret leaving Salamba at all?'

'Not in the slightest. Although there was one thing which I had to leave behind that I do regret,' confessed Moriba.

'Whatever could that have been?'

'My penis,' Moriba said, with an emphatic nod of his head.

'Your what? Good heavens, man, do you mean to say that they mutilated you?' Grunwald's eyes were wide with horror.

'Not at all,' grinned Moriba. 'I assure you that I am in full working order. But what would you say if I told you that I had a second penis, but I was obliged to leave it back in Salamba?'

Grunwald looked puzzled, and Moriba was obviously amused at his confusion.

'What's more, it wasn't any ordinary penis. I tell you, it was made of solid gold. And as big as that.' Moriba spread his arms to convey the extent of the missing member. 'I hated having to leave it behind, but it weighed a ton, and there was no way that I could have got it out of the country.'

'Really? Are you serious, or is this some sort of fantastic story that you have dreamed up?'

'It's absolutely true: an archaeological treasure of some kind which turned up just before the revolution. Think what it must be worth! Maybe one day I shall have the chance to go back and get my hands on it. Still, for now I shall have to make do with the paltry amount of money in my account here, and whatever I can graft in Rome.'

'I would not describe your balance as paltry,' Grunwald protested. 'By any standard, it is a very substantial sum and the bank has gone to great pains to look after your interests and invest wisely for you.'

Moriba laughed. 'You and your bank have not done badly out of my business, so don't pretend that you are a charitable institution, or I shall remove my account to another bank. I don't mind robbers, but I do object to hypocrites.'

Grunwald knew Moriba too well to rise to the bait. 'You will have your little joke,' he answered, but there was no humour in his smile. 'Tell me more about this extraordinary golden phallus which you say that you came across in Salamba.'

'There's nothing more to tell. It was rumoured to be part of some ancient statue which was found in a mine where it had obviously been hidden. I suppose that Milos, our new President and former revolutionary, has got his hands on it by now. But potent sexual relics are not the sort of things which should interest a sober Swiss banker.'

'Of course not,' Grunwald hastened to agree. 'It was simply curiosity on my part at such a strange story.'

However, no sooner had Moriba taken his leave than Grunwald picked up the phone and put through a call to a number in Bali. He sat, motionless and staring fixedly before him, until he was put through.

Then, speaking in almost a whisper, as if he were afraid that he would be overheard, he said, 'Isis, you know who is speaking. That for which we search has come to light. You must meet me in Salamba in one week's time. A new day is about to dawn for Osiris.'

In Ibari, the capital of Salamba, the presidential Rolls-Royce, an impressive golden sedan, swept through the gates of the palace. The sentries presented arms, and a liveried footman hurried down the steps to open the door of the vehicle. But it was not President Milos who climbed out, but a strikingly beautiful woman. When Moriba had been the master of the country, Anna had been his mistress: with his downfall, she had not hesitated for a moment before transferring her affections to his successor.

Her father had been a Swedish archaeologist who had passed rapidly through Salamba, but had dallied long enough to make a local girl pregnant. The unusual combination led to a wonderfully exotic offspring: dusky-skinned but blue-eyed, and with the delicate beauty of a tropical flower, Anna's feminine charm belied her character – calculating, cunning and as hard as nails. And in bed, she was a supreme artist who could play on the weaknesses of men, as a great musician might perform on his instrument.

23

She found Milos dictating a memorandum to a secretary. He finished quickly and the two of them retreated into one of the private rooms of the palace. Milos appeared to be preoccupied, as if he had something on his mind and was disinclined to talk. Anna was far too intelligent to press unwelcome questions or conversation: she knew how to be patient. At bedtime, she had always been able to coax their secrets from her lovers, willingly or otherwise. Nevertheless, she was concerned, since Milos was not usually a moody man.

Eventually, the two of them mounted the grand ceremonial staircase and retired to their bedroom suite. Anna withdrew into her dressing-room, undressed, and carefully selected from her wardrobe the most provocative nightdress, a mere wisp of cream-coloured nylon. She brushed her hair and applied a touch of her favourite perfume before going back into the bedroom. She dimmed the lights and switched on a stereo so that dreamy, romantic music wafted through the room.

Milos was already lying in the vast, circular bed, and Anna climbed in and snuggled up beside him. She gently stroked his back, but he remained quite inert. He had a good, chunky body and closely cropped black hair; he was a man who was immediately attractive to women and who deservedly enjoyed a high reputation as an exuberant lover. Anna let her fingers play against his firm flesh and, after a while, he began to stir. She nibbled on his ear and he grunted in satisfaction. But when he turned to face her, Anna was astonished to find that this great stud did not even sport a worthwhile erection. Something was definitely wrong.

But Anna had never allowed any man to withstand her sexual assault and she got to work on her prey. She wriggled down in the bed until she could take his flaccid cock in her mouth, and she started to work harder than she had ever worked before. At last the great lollipop grew stiff and Milos's hands caressed her hair as she felt him become responsive to her. But he still did nothing to take the initiative, although on other occasions his behaviour vied with that of a raging bull.

Suddenly, he grabbed her by her hair and pulled her up. Pushing her onto her back, Milos climbed over her body, and without any gesture of warmth or affection, thrust into her with short, hard strokes. Anna held him in her arms and pressed her lips against his. His kiss was grudging: it was as though her body was unwelcome to him but he found it impossible to resist her overwhelming sensuality. He approached his climax without any of his normal carefree joy and he did nothing to try to give her pleasure. She had never considered him to be a selfish lover, but on this occasion he simply used her body as if it were an inanimate object, and emptied his semen into her.

Anna went into the bathroom and washed herself thoroughly. She felt soiled, not by sex, but by the indifference of her man. When she came back into the bedroom, Milos was lying on his back, gazing blankly at the ceiling.

'It wasn't any good, was it,' he muttered.

'I suppose that you were thinking of some other woman,' Anna said mockingly.

She was confident that there was not another woman in Africa, from Cairo to the Cape, who could stand comparison with her for the sheer power of her sexuality. She was absolutely right.

And yet, the image of another woman did indeed haunt Milos's imagination. A mere girl, who had been a passenger on a plane which he had hijacked and who, inexplicably, had helped him to escape when the coup had gone wrong. They had hardly met, but she had clearly felt a great attraction to him. He had shrugged off the episode, but he could not dismiss it from his mind. A Scots girl, a cabaret singer, that he remembered, but it took some effort to recall her name. Sandy something or other was all he recollected, but the memory of her blonde good looks, the way she smiled and the liveliness of her violet eyes was as vivid as if she, and not his mistress, had just shared his bed. So, Milos did not reply to Anna's taunt.

'This place is under a curse,' Anna complained. 'I warned you that this would happen.'

'What are you talking about?' Milos demanded.

'You know well enough.' Anna's tone was accusing. 'I told you about that fantastic golden cock which the American mining engineer found.'

'You mean that man you were living with under orders from your master, Moriba,' Milos sneered.

'He could teach you a lot,' Anna flared up. 'And when the golden cock was in the room, it was marvellous. Every time we made love, it was a miracle. The thing was some sort of magic. And now!'

She did not need to finish the sentence, but glared at Milos contemptuously.

'Superstitious nonsense!' Milos retorted.

'If it is such nonsense, why is it that ever since that golden phallus of some old god was taken out of Salamba, you have never been able to perform decently?'

'I have a lot on my mind,' Milos protested. 'After all, I am the President of this country.'

The scorn in Anna's eyes was sufficient answer, and Milos felt his temper rising.

'I thought that you were after the damned thing because it was worth so much money,' he accused.

'So I was at first,' Anna replied. 'Then I discovered the sexual potency of the divine penis, but it was too late. You let Moriba slip through your fingers so that he was able to get out of Salamba and smuggle it out with him. You may be the President, but with that sceptre, he is an Emperor. No woman can resist him – nor any man either, for that matter. That's real power!'

'If you have such faith in this Golden Phallus of Osiris, perhaps you ought to go and rejoin your one-time lover, Asi Moriba. It should not be too difficult to track him down, and with your talents, I am sure that you would be able to find an opportunity to lay your hands on the thing.'

'Are you serious?' Anna asked.

'Why not? But you had better be clear about one thing.' Milos's voice grew harsher. 'Once you have this valuable relic in your greedy little fingers, you come straight back here with it. None of your stupid tricks, Anna. Something very unpleasant would happen to you if you did anything foolish. And don't think that you could go into hiding. You know the sort of people I have who would hunt you down, wherever you went, and your precious Emperor Moriba would not be able to protect you.'

Anna shivered. She knew that Milos was not a man to make idle threats.

In London, the weather was much colder than in Ibari, but the temperature in the bedroom of Sandra Mitchell and her lover, Donald McFee, was a great deal higher than in that of Anna and Milos. They had not long got back from their eventful trip to Salamba. Donald, a member of the Scottish international football team, was enjoying a short break before resuming training with his club; Sandra, on the other hand, had just signed a contract to perform in a fashionable night club in London for the next few weeks, singing and playing the saxophone.

27

Donald was not yet twenty, but he had already achieved a legendary reputation for his skill on the football field. He was not a big man, but had a wiry resilience and was as nimble as a mountain cat. In the tiny, remote mining village where he had been brought up, he had not enjoyed much in the way of sexual adventures, but his education had been advanced during his stay in Salamba, and he still remembered with a shudder how he had been shamelessly seduced by Anna. But he adored Sandra, and he was a straightforward, uncomplicated lover who left the more imaginative variations to his partner.

They had spent the day shopping and strolling in the park, and they were pleasantly tired when they got back to their hotel. Sandra insisted that they have a rest before going out for dinner, but she knew that Donald had in mind something other than sleeping when they entered their bedroom.

'If you want to come into the same bed as me, you had better take a shower first,' Sandra told him.

'Oh come on now, Sandy, that can wait until afterwards,' Donald pleaded.

'After what?' she teased.

His answer was to take her in his arms and kiss her long and hard. She could feel the urgency of his need in the taut muscles of his body as he pressed against her, and she knew too how eagerly she wanted him. But when he released her, she persisted in driving him into the bathroom, as much to prolong the pleasure of her own anticipation as to tantalize him by making him wait. However, as a reward for his good behaviour, while he was in the shower, she slipped out of her clothes and joined him, just to soap his back she assured him. Under the gushing stream of hot water, they engaged in the most enjoyable of all aquatic sports. Squirming like a passionate eel, Donald managed to turn to face his sweet tormentor, and they indulged in a mutual body massage. Sandra's fingers rippled over his skin, adding a new edge to his desire. Donald's ministrations were somewhat brisker, as if to emphasize his impatience to put an end to these preliminaries. When Sandra gently soaped his testicles, he protested volubly at his treatment, although it was obvious that his discomfort was combined with an exquisite enjoyment. But finally, Sandra yielded before his ultimate threat that he would come in the shower and be too exhausted to be any use to her once they got into bed.

'You would not love me if you thought that I permitted grubby men between my sheets, now would you?' Sandra pointed out, as she folded a thick, warm towel around his body.

'I was not grubby,' Donald exclaimed indignantly.

He grabbed another towel, and wrapping it around Sandra, proceeded to rub her down with a vigour which seemed to express his resentment.

'I think that you still had some African mud on you,' she mocked him.

They carried on this pretence of an argument while they dried themselves. Then Sandra interrupted Donald in the middle of a particularly high-flown phrase.

'Your trouble is that you talk too much. Why don't you come to bed?'

He administered a playful smack on her bottom, as he followed her into the bedroom. But he still had to wait a little longer.

'Me first,' Sandra insisted. 'Once you have got what you want, you go all limp and useless for ages.'

Donald was ready to launch another protest, but decided that his best course was to get on with it before she thought up some fresh way of delaying his pleasure.

His mouth was warm and sweet as their tongues met

29

and, in the contact of their bodies, Donald could sense the love which she felt for him and which matched his own passion for her. Her eyes were shining, and her contented smile encouraged him to do all the things which he had learned she wanted him to do. When he let his tongue play in her ears, she purred like a cat which was being petted, but his tiny love bites on the back of her neck produced, as always from Sandra, giggles punctuated by excited gasps. Her nipples were as erect as his own straining cock, and he circled each with his tongue before taking them in his mouth and gently sucking them. Sandra, her eyes closed, clutched at his cheeks and hair and let her hands urge him to treat her more roughly, and his fingers closed firmly on her delicate, yielding flesh.

But it was when he sank his head between her thighs and lovingly parted the soft, fleshy lips to expose her hot, swollen clitoris, glistening from her welling juices, to his questing tongue that she began to sway and build up the rhythm of their love-making. Donald was drugged by the taste and the scent of her, sharp and tangy, which inflamed yet more his heightened senses and, for the instant, the urgency of his own lust was, if not forgotten, overridden.

'No, not yet,' she breathed.

But their primal dance of desire could not be checked and the couple were swept along, unable to break free or to hold themselves in check, until, with a muffled scream, Sandra succumbed to an orgasm which shook her limbs in a series of glorious spasms of sheer joy.

Now, it was Donald's turn to seek relief, and he plunged his shaft into the lush, moist paradise of her cunt. Sandra raised her legs until they were hooked behind those of Donald and strained, as if to sink him even further into the very depths of her. She cupped his balls in her hand, and felt them contract as the sperm mounted inside her lover's driving penis. Donald was panting, and their mouths met in a savage embrace. From his lips, Sandra drank in her own juices, and the sensation intensified the crescendo of their coupling.

Instinctively, Donald knew that the moment had arrived and that Sandra was ready for one more fantastic explosion. He drove faster and deeper, and she moved with him as one person, or one animal – 'the beast with two backs'. She ached for their climax, and yet at the same time wished that they could keep on going for ever. But her excitement mounted to such a pitch that she knew that she would go crazy if it lasted one second longer. At that very moment, Donald seemed to burst inside her, and the violence of his ejaculation caused her to come with him in an even more uncontrollable eruption.

Absolutely exhausted physically and drained emotionally, they subsided in the soaked, ruffled sheets, and slowly returned to the everyday world. For quite a long time, Donald clasped her in their golden afterglow. At last, they parted reluctantly, but the spell lingered on.

'I guess that now both of us really do need to take a bath,' Donald commented.

'You are so unromantic,' chuckled Sandra, and kissed him tenderly on the tip of his nose.

But she got out of the bed and walked into the bathroom. Donald heard the water beginning to fill the tub, and he lethargically went to join her.

'You know, I don't think that it has ever been better than that,' he told her.

Sandra nodded happily. 'Don't laugh at me, but I feel as if there has been a sort of new magic whenever we make love, ever since we have had that odd bit of metal in the room.'

'That's no way to refer to the solid gold penis of a god,' Donald grinned. 'But I know what you mean: it does make you feel that it exercises an eerie kind of influence. I've felt it before. However, we shall have to give it back to that French archaeologist, now that he has managed to get out of Salamba.'

Professor Louis Halevy had been summoned to Salamba to examine the Golden Phallus by the American mining engineer to whom a native worker had brought it. He had been detained and repeatedly searched by Milos's police, who had finally concluded that Moriba had left with the ancient relic, and so, that same week, they had allowed the Frenchman to return to Europe.

In the other room, the Golden Phallus of Osiris, which Sandra had smuggled out of the country, concealed in her saxophone, was lying on the bedside table where it had been casually tossed by her before they made love.

There certainly was a mysterious aura about the strange object which was destined to exert so powerful an attraction over so many people in the coming months.

# 3

## Snakes in the Grass

In the presidential palace, Anna gave vent to her annoyance. She glared at Milos across the table on which there
were the remnants of their breakfast.

'I don't understand why you have to see this little Swiss
creep. It's not as though he were an ambassador or a
visiting Pope. Some shopkeeper from the Alps calls your
private secretary, and you agree to give him an immediate
audience. He probably wants to sell you a cuckoo clock:
what sort of a president are you?'

Milos snorted. 'Don't be ridiculous. I told you, he is
the director of one of the most important banks in the
world. I have to see him.'

'You never have any time for me, except when you
want to fuck. And that has not been such a world-
shattering event lately. Why can't this guy make an
appointment in the usual way? What does he want,
anyway?'

'How the hell do I know before I see him! Have you
got no sense at all, woman? Salamba has borrowed
billions from international banks, and more from this
Swiss bank than any other.'

'Well, if he is going to talk about money, why does
he have to bother you instead of seeing your Finance
Minister?'

'I suppose that, after our revolution, they are nervous
and want to see the boss to make sure that their money is
safe. If they were to pull out their loan, the country
would be in trouble. I might even lose my job: you
certainly would lose yours,' he sneered.

33

Anna was not entirely convinced. 'Maybe I ought to be with you when you see him.'

'That would be about as helpful as dropping an atom bomb on the palace,' Milos retorted. 'Do you honestly believe that the way to reassure a conservative banker from Europe that his money is not being wasted is for him to be received by the President's expensive mistress? Keep well out of the way: why don't you go into town and buy yourself a new hat to keep the sun off what few brains you do have?'

Anna stormed out of the room, and Milos composed himself to receive his unwelcome but influential visitor.

But when Josef Grunwald was ushered into his presence, Milos was surprised to find that he was accompanied by an unexpected escort. The woman who was known as Isis, even when she was not wearing her awesome, priestly regalia, made a remarkable impression. She stared fixedly at Milos while Grunwald spoke.

'Mr President, may I first congratulate you on your accession to power and on ridding your country of that loathsome dictator, Asi Moriba. I am sure that I speak for the whole banking community when I say that we feel that our investment in Salamba is at last in reliable hands.'

Milos nodded, and was about to express his appreciation, but there was some elusive quality in the way that the woman held his eye which prevented him from speaking.

Grunwald continued with treacly self-assurance. 'However, something has come to my attention which, if we do not deal with the matter tactfully and expeditiously, I fear could sour these good relations, and I am sure that you do not need me to spell out to you the difficulties which your country would encounter in those circumstances.'

Milos stiffened as he reacted to the implicit threat, but he was still inexplicably unable to find his voice.

'So I have come to see you in this informal manner in order to resolve this development, before it has a chance to become a problem.'

He favoured the President with a kindly smile: Isis's expression did not alter. Her unblinking, basilisk stare held the President of Salamba helplessly mute.

'I have become aware that a priceless relic has been discovered in Salamba and it is our mission' – he turned his head towards Isis to include her – 'to restore it to its rightful owners. You know, of course, to what I am referring. I assume that the Golden Phallus of Osiris is being held for safe custody somewhere inside this palace. Will you please produce it for us.'

Milos shook his head.

Grunwald sighed. 'I see that we shall have to stage a little demonstration to bring you to reason. It might also give you an interesting insight into the enormous psychological powers which are at our disposal.'

While he was speaking, Isis drew a faded sheet of papyrus from a small cedarwood box which she had been carrying, and began to read from it. Milos listened, fascinated, although he did not understand one word of what she chanted. It was as if the relentless monotone of her vibrant, rich voice was boring into his brain, stifling his senses and paralysing his will and his reason. Under its influence, He became aware of a gradual change taking place all around him.

The walls of the room appeared to retreat, and the very air which he breathed was subtly different. He was in what appeared to be a cavern, or perhaps a temple. It was dark, but he could still see Isis, whose figure glowed as if she had been bathed in phosphorus. How it came about that she was now naked he could not fathom, but in his mind, and in his loins, he realized that she was the most desirable woman he had ever seen. He ached unbearably to take her in his arms and possess her, yet he was powerless to move a muscle.

Suddenly, she was no longer alone. The man who stood beside her was Josef Grunwald, and at the same time, it was not. For this was a bronzed Grunwald, rejuvenated, taller, stronger, more masculine than the pasty-faced, plump, plain banker, a character at once heroic and as charismatic as his mystic partner, whose voice continued to bewitch Milos.

This idealized Grunwald, also nude, confronted him and shamelessly displayed his enormous cock. Long, thick and smooth, it was a symbol of authority to Milos, and his mouth watered as he imagined himself tasting its savoury sweetness.

They did not move, but Milos now saw that Grunwald had penetrated Isis. They stood facing each other, and in his own flesh, Milos felt their sinuous movements. While his body was swept by the ecstasy and the anguish of their union, their faces remained blank, expressionless masks. Milos had no notion of how long they stood there. To his wondering gaze they remained as cold and immobile as statues, while his own body was racked by the burning fever of their love-making, and he knew from the quaking of his own penis the moment when Grunwald had implanted his semen in the body of the priestess.

Still that voice continued to dominate his consciousness, but now he had joined the two supernatural figures, again without any sensation of having physically moved. He was kneeling before them, and Isis parted her legs so that he could lick from her brimming cunt the sperm of Grunwald which was trickling down her legs. She accepted his tribute with the cold aloofness of a superior being, as though he were a dog or a cat who was rubbing himself against his mistress. But as he sucked and kissed, he found that his lips were closed, not against the softness of her labia, but around the firm fullness of Grunwald's phallus, once more fully distended. It filled his mouth, almost choking him, as he attempted to swallow. Milos had never before in his life experienced the slightest homosexual attraction, but it was as if the gratification of this haughtily remote male was the culmination of all his sexual desires. The great cock was iron-hard, and its piston strokes slammed his head backwards and forwards. It seemed to be growing bigger every second; it possessed not simply his thirsting mouth, but his entire being.

Beneath this pitiless onslaught, Milos felt himself growing weak and the world was becoming dark. He was on the verge of fainting, and his hands clawed desperately to hold on to the buttocks of Grunwald, but they met with empty air. Then, sperm was pumping into his mouth, salt and sticky, and he gulped spasmodically like a drowning man. At the same time, Milos felt his own pants being soaked, as his own orgasm came upon him. It was sudden and unexpected, for he had not been conscious of what was happening to his own body while he had been serving those of Isis and Grunwald. He crumpled up and, with a strained whimper, collapsed at the feet of his subjugators.

The incantation of Isis ceased, and Milos opened his eyes. Sure enough, he was lying on the ground, but the other two were standing, fully clothed and apparently unaffected by the furious storm which had assailed his senses. They looked down at him, as though it were the most natural thing in the world for the president of a country to masturbate and prostrate himself before them.

Isis carefully folded the sheet of papyrus and put it back in its box. Grunwald cleared his throat.

'I trust that what has just occurred will have convinced

37

you that we are serious and also that we are the people to whom the Golden Phallus should be restored.'

Slowly, Milos regained his self-control. He had scrambled to his feet and dabbed his saturated crotch with a handkerchief. Now that Isis had become silent, he found that he was once more able to speak.

'It is not here.'

Grunwald stared at him stonily, but Isis intervened.

'He is speaking the truth. I can tell when a man is lying.'

The banker's lips tightened, but he nodded acceptance of her statement.

'Since you have indicated that it is not in the palace, please tell us where you have hidden it and make the necessary arrangements to surrender it to us.'

'I tell you that it is not in my possession. That gorilla, Moriba, carried it off with him when he fled the country.'

'That cannot be.' Grunwald's tone was authoritative. 'We have examined Moriba and he has assured us that this precious fragment of the god's body remains in Salamba.'

'And I can assure you that it does not,' replied Milos.

They stood in silence. Isis looked long and hard into Milos's eyes, and then turned to Grunwald.

'It is as he says. We must seek it elsewhere.'

'You are not the only people who want to find it,' Milos told them, thinking of Anna's frenzied obsession. 'Who are you, anyway?'

They ignored his question. 'If you recover this object, you must give it to us,' Grunwald told him.

'Why should I?' Milos felt his old confidence coming back. After all, if his mysterious visitors had journeyed across the world to find the Golden Phallus in Salamba, it was obvious that they were fallible, so their apparently superhuman powers did not necessarily render them invincible. 'I rather think that it would be in Salamba's interests to retain the phallus, once it is back in our hands. Since it is clearly unique, it would be a great asset to our tourist trade.'

Grunwald was on the point of contradicting Milos, but once more he was silenced by Isis who took the initiative.

'There is no reason for us to quarrel. You must know that the phallus is only one part of the great golden statue of Osiris. We are members of the sect of Isis. We worship the goddess who has entrusted us with the secrets of sexuality with which we can enslave men and women, as you have just witnessed. Already, we have in our possession some other fragments of the statue, and it is our aim to restore it in its entirety. But the phallus is the greatest prize. We must find it, now that it has come to light. As for you, I make you a proposition. The cult of Isis needs a shrine for the statue. Why not Salamba? If we let it fall into the hands of the Egyptians or one of the Western countries, they would confine it in some dusty museum. But we want a living temple where men and women from every country can come and adore Isis and Osiris, somewhere where they can experience their living power, not stare at a dead piece of sculpture behind a glass screen. You want to encourage tourism in your country, but what have you to offer? Just think how different it would be if Salamba were to be the centre of a world religion. And what a religion! One based on love – not spiritual love, but real, carnal knowledge and the most complete awareness of the enjoyment of the flesh that exists anywhere in the world. Ibari would attract more pilgrims than Jerusalem, Mecca and Rome added together. What do you think of that?'

Milos pondered, then his face broke into a broad smile.

'Why not! The first thing we have to do is to recover the phallus, and for that we might as well join our forces. There is an important material consideration to be reckoned with, however. I can offer you the sanctuary you seek for the statue and for your cult. The wealth which should be attracted to the sect and to this country could be enormous. I feel that it would be appropriate for a percentage to be reserved for the personal account of the President of that country which extends this hospitality, don't you?'

'We would have no objection to such an arrangement,' said Isis.

Josef Grunwald's eyes lit up, and for the first time he exhibited genuine enthusiasm.

'Now you are beginning to speak a language which I understand,' he beamed.

A stone's throw from the Via Condotti, and Rome's most fashionable boutiques and exclusive couturiers, there is a run-down alley which is rarely visited by either tourists or the police. The grimy plaster is peeling off the walls of the tall, ramshackle buildings: several of the windows are broken and those which survive have not been washed for decades. Many of the rooms are occupied by whole families, and during the day the shouting, screaming and chattering of children echo through the confined space, and the stale air is rank and heavy from the steam and the smell from the primitive kitchens.

At night, there is a completely different kind of animation. In one of the upper-storey garrets, Emilia Ferruci was getting ready for work. In her late thirties, she had the careworn face of a woman ten years older. Her hair had been a defiant, flaming red, but it was beginning to grow thinner and lank. Her cheekbones were pronounced, giving her features a gauntness which cosmetics did little to relieve. Rinsing herself in tepid water in the cracked, brown, stained basin, Emilia glanced at herself in the blotched mirror, and squinted her disapproval. Her scraggy breasts swung limply, like half-empty wine-skins, and she languidly squeezed the pus from a blackhead on her shoulder blade. Still, she reflected, my legs aren't at all bad: thanks to them, I can still hook in a man or two. There was a hole in her tights, but Emilia judged that it was too small to matter, and she hitched up her vivid scarlet, but slightly soiled, miniskirt, pulled on a worn tank top and, picking up her sequined vanity bag, went back into her studio bedroom. She tidied the bedclothes, threw a dirty blouse into a cupboard, slipped on a pair of shoes with heels like miniature stilts, and tottered out on to the landing and down the rickety, uncarpeted wooden stairs.

Some of the more favoured girls had a regular pitch, perhaps a street corner near a popular restaurant or one of the tourist spots. Emilia was less fortunate, but she had a beat which she walked, loitering in the more promising areas for as long as possible. Approaching the Via Condotti, she cast an enquiring glance at a couple of men, but one scowled at her and the other did not even appear to notice her as he walked past. It was going to be another bloody awful night, she concluded.

A gigantic black man was striding towards her. Emilia hesitated. A lot of the girls would not go with black men because they said that they were too well-developed and that could be painful. Emilia could not afford to be particular. Unhappily, she smiled encouragingly at Asi Moriba.

The former dictator gave her an appraising look and nodded assent. Emilia turned and led the way back to her pad. It was unusual for a man not to ask the price before going with her, but this big fellow did not utter one word until they were in her room. He seemed very sure of himself, and Emilia was a bit uneasy in case all he wanted was to beat her up. Still, Giuseppe would be downstairs, and if the worst happened, she could rely on him to be up in her room in a flash, in order to protect his property. After all, she was a source of income for him.

She wondered for how much she could hit this pigeon. He was well dressed and might have come from the States, so perhaps he did not know the going rate in Rome. He looked around the sparsely furnished room, but his expression did not indicate what he thought of this love nest. Emilia tossed her tiny bag onto a table, and addressed him in faltering English.

'OK, big boy. You tell me. You got dollars?'

Moriba grinned and nodded.

'So this little trick costs fifty bucks, without any fancy extras. Is that what you want, or are you after something special?'

Moriba did not reply, but produced a wad of dollar bills. He threw some on the table, apparently without bothering to count them. Emilia picked them up. There was a hundred and fifty dollars, and she stuffed them hastily into her bag. She pulled off her clothes and walked towards the bathroom.

'I won't be more than a couple of minutes,' she assured her affluent client. 'Make yourself comfortable.'

She was astonished to find, when she returned, that he was still standing, fully dressed, where she had left him.

'What's the matter with you?' she demanded. 'Are you shy? I thought that you would be in bed by now.'

Moriba spoke for the first time since they had met.

'I don't want to go to bed with you,' he informed her.

There was a deprecatory tone to his voice which stung her as if he had slapped her face.

'So what do you want then?' she flared up. 'You're not

getting your money back you know, just because you have changed your mind.'

'I haven't changed my mind,' Moriba laughed. 'I never had the slightest intention of touching you.'

'So what do you want?' she repeated.

Something very close to panic mounted in her throat. He was so massive, so powerful, and there was a veiled menace in his insolent indifference to her.

'Send for your man,' he ordered.

'What?'

She gazed at him in bewilderment. If he were gay, why had he not picked up a boy? God knows, there were enough of them about.

'Your man, your pimp.' He was talking to her as though she were a backward child. 'There's no way that an old hag like you could have hung on in Rome without having a man behind you. I want to talk to him.'

'You are out of your mind,' she cried. 'He would kill you.'

'I'll take the risk.' Moriba smiled grimly. 'Now, are you going to send for him, or do I have to hurt you to persuade you?'

Emilia cocked her head to one side like a sagacious owl upbraiding a rash nestling.

'Don't blame me for what happens,' she smirked, and rapped three times on the floor.

Giuseppe must have been waiting. He had his own key, and within seconds he had burst into the room. He went to spring on Moriba, but Emilia stopped him.

'It's all right. I'm not hurt and he isn't threatening me.'

Giuseppe stared uncertainly at the stranger. He was a strong, hairy, barrel-chested man whose brawn greatly exceeded his brains. His normal response to any problem was to settle it with his fist, unless it was serious enough to require more drastic treatment.

'What's going on?' he growled.

'I need to meet the boss,' Moriba told him calmly. 'And before you tell me that you don't know what I am talking about, let me say that I am fully aware that this part of Rome is not controlled by the Mafia, but that there is a local guy who has quite a big area. You would not be allowed to operate without his approval, so you must be able to get me to see him. Do it!'

'You're a cop, a bleeding pig,' sneered Giuseppe. 'Get the hell out of here.'

'I have been in that line of business,' Moriba agreed cordially, 'but that was in the past and a long way from Rome. I promise you that I have no contact with the forces of law and order. Quite the opposite: I have a deal to propose.'

'What sort of a deal?' Giuseppe's tone was defiant and suspicious.

'That I discuss with the boss, not with any hood from the street. And let me warn you,' Moriba added in the same even tone of voice, 'that if you try to pull that knife which is up your sleeve, I shall break your arm.'

With roar of rage, Giuseppe hurled himself at Moriba, only to receive a crashing blow in his face which sent him reeling across the room. Before he could recover, or Emilia had a chance to intervene, Moriba had followed up his advantage with a hefty kick in the Italian's crotch. Giuseppe doubled up and squealed in agony.

'You needed a lesson in manners,' Moriba told him. 'And now, you should realize that I am serious. If Pino Astoli is still running the show, I want to see him. You fix it. Meet me tomorrow at midday outside Santa Maria sopre Minerva. And don't be late, or next time I won't be so gentle and you'll be a hospital case.'

Moriba strode out of the apartment and they heard his steps clatter down the stairs.

'Who is this man and how can it be possible that he knows of Astoli?' Emilia asked fearfully.

Giuseppe was still groaning on the floor. He shook his head angrily. Later, when he had recovered from the excruciating pain which Moriba had inflicted on him, he beat the living shit out of Emilia for bringing back so evil a character.

The church of Santa Maria sopre Minerva stands close to the Pantheon. In front of it is a curious sort of obelisk in the form of a tall column on the back of an elephant. Punctually at noon the following day, Asi Moriba was standing regarding this object when Giuseppe sidled up to him. With a flick of his head, he indicated that Moriba should follow him, and he led the way through the crowded streets until they reached a busy taverna.

The two of them shouldered their way across the bustling restaurant, and Giuseppe went to usher Moriba through a door into the private rooms beyond. Moriba shook his head.

'I'll wait here, sonny, where there are a lot of other people. You go in and tell my old pal, Pino, to come and join me.'

Giuseppe did not intend to argue again with this wild man, but an ugly leer flickered over his features.

'Scared?' he mocked.

'Just cautious,' Moriba answered. 'Now, move!'

He took a seat at a corner table. A waiter hurried over and told him that the table was reserved.

'Well, now it is unreserved,' Moriba informed him.

The waiter glanced for a second at the mass of muscle before him and moved away. Moriba, absolutely untroubled, waited for perhaps five minutes. Then Giuseppe returned, accompanied by a thick-set, stubbly chinned man whose eyes were hidden by heavy dark glasses. Behind him, like a couple of hunting dogs, stalked two heavily built bodyguards. Pino Astoli stared at the intruder. Then his face broke into a broad smile.

'I might have guessed that it would be you,' he chuckled.

Moriba looked coldly at Giuseppe.

'Beat it,' he commanded. 'And take those morons with you.'

The three toughs looked at their boss, but Astoli shooed them away.

'Nobody is going to start anything in the middle of this crowd,' he assured them. 'And this gentleman is well known to me.'

'Gentleman!' grunted Giuseppe disgustedly, but he and the other pair quickly made themselves scarce.

'So, the great Moriba has arrived in Rome,' commented the underworld boss with a dry smile. 'And what are you going to do here?'

'Take over your operation,' Moriba replied unhesitatingly.

Astoli raised his eyebrows in surprised disbelief.

'Don't worry, you will be well taken care of,' Moriba told him. 'I need girls, lots of girls, and I know that you collect these country kids who come into Rome, hoping to make it in movies, and ending up on the streets. That, my friend, is a dreadful waste. I can dispose of them at higher prices than you have ever dreamed of.'

'I'm happy with what we make now,' Astoli rasped.

'Well, I am not,' Moriba countered emphatically. 'You remember how much the Arabs used to pay for a white girl, especially if she were a blonde. Salamba has become suddenly rich with all those minerals that the Americans are digging up, and the boys back there will give double what was paid in the Middle East.'

'Very interesting.' Astoli's voice was as cold as ice.

46

'But aren't you forgetting that you don't happen to be in charge in Salamba any more?'

'I still have all the contacts. You have the girls: I have the customers. Don't worry, I'll let you have a decent share of what we take. In fact, you will find that I am quite generous, that is if you are sensible. Remember, girls are much easier to find than the sort of customers I have.'

There was a long pause, during which the two men looked steadily at each other. Then, Astoli got to his feet.

'I'll think about it and let you know,' he said.

'Don't think for too long, otherwise things will start to happen,' Moriba warned him. 'You can find me at the Hassler.'

'Naturally. I would have assumed that you would stay at the best hotel in the city.'

Pino Astoli turned to leave. Moriba touched him lightly on the sleeve.

'Are you still going with that pretty French girl? What was her name now, Monique Dubuffet, wasn't it? It would be a pity if she were to get hurt as a result of a silly business misunderstanding, don't you agree?'

Astoli's eyes shone with fury.

'I'll kill you if you try and touch her, do you understand?'

Moriba laughed.

'Don't take too long to make up your mind now, will you.'


Anna never did find out how Moriba managed to evade the censorship and get his letter delivered to her in Ibari. Presumably, even after his flight, enough of the men he had left behind remained loyal for him to keep in being some kind of underground organization. But there it was, a peremptory summons to her to join him in Rome without delay.

She had become unhappy with her liaison with Milos; their sex life showed no signs of improving and, since the arrival of the Swiss banker and his mysterious companion, her dissatisfaction had grown. Milos had become even more moody and introspective and, despite her bedroom tactics, she had been unable to worm out of him the real reason for their prolonged visit. She had noticed, however, that whenever she mentioned the Golden Phallus, Milos became even more taciturn, and swiftly changed the subject. Anna continued to believe that the object had strange sexual powers, and that it remained in the possession of Moriba. Milos made no effort to disillusion her.

So when she received Moriba's letter, she decided at once that she would comply with his demand. But what should she tell Milos? If she tried to bolt without his knowledge, she might well get caught attempting to cross the frontier, and she dreaded to think what sort of revenge Milos might then exact. On the other hand, if she told him of her plan, he would be able to trace Moriba's whereabouts, if necessary by having her followed, and his men might then liquidate the former police chief before she could steal from him the all-important Golden Phallus.

Her quandary was resolved in an altogether unexpected manner. She had gone out one day, intending to spend the afternoon with the girlfriend of a Swedish doctor. When she arrived at her villa, Anna was told that the couple were taking an unplanned vacation in Stockholm, so she returned unexpectedly to the presidential palace. She hurried up the ceremonial staircase and pushed open the door of their bedroom suite. A bizarre spectacle met her eyes.

Reclining on the bed was the woman they called Isis. She seemed to be mumbling some words which she was reading from a document written on an old piece of papyrus. She had removed her panties and tights, and Milos and Grunwald crouched on the floor at her feet. Although the two men looked directly at Anna, she was certain that they did not see her. Each of them in turn was licking the woman's arse and cunt with an unearthly concentration. Anna stared in disbelief for a brief moment. She felt her own senses becoming drowsy at the sound of the strange chant, but such was her indignation that she stormed out of the room before it could establish any pronounced influence over her. How was it, she wondered, that while her own sexual relations with Milos remained so pathetic, he could be ready behind her back to indulge in this mini-orgy with Isis and with that podgy, unattractive little man?

She confronted Milos that night in their bedroom, telling him what she had witnessed. He seemed totally unrepentant and made no comment on the scene.

'Since you are obviously having a kinky affair with that woman, I think that I shall go away for a few days. It's no fun for me here now.'

'Where will you go?' asked Milos.

'Europe. Probably Paris. It will give you a chance to work this thing out of your system, and I shall enjoy a break. You never know, I might even find a lover of my own.'

Milos shrugged his shoulders. 'Do whatever you like. Now, turn out the light and let's get some sleep. I have to make an early start tomorrow.'

Anna was astounded at how easily she had obtained her freedom. But she was displeased by Milos's casualness. Since the arrival of Isis, so voluptuous yet so aloof, he had become another man, no longer responsive to

Anna's sexual domination. Undoubtedly, the time had come for her to change partners.

At Ibari's international airport, a few days later, Anna boarded a plane bound for Paris from where she could easily take a connecting flight to Rome. If she had paid attention to the people who were jostling their way out of the airport after the arrival of flights from London and New York, she might have noticed among others a formally dressed man of distinguished appearance and a good-looking American woman. Cleo Janis and Andrew Drummond, along with the other members of the caucus which directed the affairs of the cult of Isis, had come to hold meetings with their new sponsor.

'There is a lady asking for you in reception,' the clerk told Moriba over the house phone.

Moriba was surprised. He reckoned that it was too soon for Anna to have escaped from Salamba, and he was not expecting any other visitor.

'Is she alone?'

'Yes, sir.'

'Send her up.'

Despite the reception clerk's assurance, Moriba was not taking any chances. Both the salon and the bedroom of suites in the Hassler have doors giving onto the outside corridor, and while the woman was pressing the buzzer outside one door, Moriba was peering out through the other which he had opened a fraction. Satisfied that she really was on her own, he let her in.

He hardly recognized Emilia. Her clothes were clean and respectable and she had clearly taken great pains over her make-up. She was not by any stretch of the imagination a lovely woman, but she would have looked pleasant enough if only her face had not been heavily bruised and one of her eyes blackened and puffy. Moriba did not waste time with formalities.

'What do you want?'

'I've come to warn you.' Her tone was factual and undramatic. 'Astoli has sent Giuseppe to kill you.'

Moriba yawned. 'Of course. That's the only way he could react. But why are you telling me this?'

She answered him by pointing to her ravaged face. 'And,' she added, 'you are the only man who has ever given me money without taking something in return. Even more money than I asked.'

'How did you know where to find me?'

'I was there when Astoli gave Giuseppe his orders. The sexist bastards treat women like shit. They think that I am stupid, so they speak in front of me, as if I was a piece of furniture in the room, without eyes or ears.'

Moriba nodded. He approved of the vehemence which gave Emilia's voice an unaccustomed sharpness, and he knew that she was fully aware of the risk that she had taken in coming to put him on his guard, at once a gesture of defiance and a cry for revenge.

'You can tell me where I can find Astoli and one or two other people.'

She was useful. She knew where everybody lived, which bars they frequented, and where they habitually hung out during the days and the nights. He carefully took down the information she gave him. Then he put away his notebook.

'Don't come to the hotel again: it is too dangerous,' he told her. 'You will be able to contact me here.'

He scribbled an address in Trastevere on a scrap of paper and handed it to her. She read it carefully, repeated it several times to herself, and then tore up the paper.

'Anybody might go over my pockets or my purse,' she explained.

'You had better be on your way. I don't want you to be about when your boyfriend comes to pay me his social call. Go out through the tradesmen's entrance, in case they are already watching the hotel. Come to that address tomorrow evening at ten.'

She buttoned her coat, nodded her agreement, and left the suite without saying another word.

Moriba had to wait for a couple of hours before Giuseppe showed up. He called on the house phone and told Moriba that Astoli had decided to go along with his proposition and that he had a car waiting outside to take Moriba to a rendezvous with his boss.

'I'll be right down. Wait for me in the lobby,' Moriba said.

The car had been parked at the foot of the Spanish Steps, the Scala degli Spagni, well away from the hotel entrance which is situated at the top of the great stone steps. Giuseppe's three companions were lounging nearby. They considered that Moriba might prove unwilling to get into a car in which there was already seated a full execution squad. Once he was inside, they would close in before he could make his escape. At any rate, that was the plan.

Moriba emerged from the elevator with a nonchalant grin.

'Feeling better today?' he asked Giuseppe solicitously.

Giuseppe favoured him with an amiable scowl. 'Seems that you are a special friend of the boss. He has told me to take great care of you.'

He led the way across the lobby, but Moriba slapped his pocket and halted.

'I'm right out of cigarettes. Why don't you go on ahead and I'll meet you in the street.'

Giuseppe was not the intellectual star in Astoli's firmament, but he had been taught that you never let a mark out of your sight. He offered Moriba an opened pack from his own pocket.

'I don't smoke that Italian shit,' Moriba told him scornfully. 'I'm going to get some Marlboros. There's a kiosk which sells American brands right at the back of the hotel.'

He began to walk back across the lobby, but Giuseppe protested.

'Say, man, we can pick up some on the road. I can't leave the car for long where it is parked.'

'So Astoli will pick up your parking ticket,' Moriba called. 'I shan't be long.'

'I'll come with you,' Giuseppe cried desperately. 'But that's not the way out: where are you going?'

'I told you. The kiosk is behind the hotel. It's quicker to go out through the back entrance.'

And Moriba strode along the service corridor and out of the rear door of the hotel, with Giuseppe trotting to keep up with him. They found themselves in a narrow, deserted back street which Moriba had carefully reconnoitred while he waited for Giuseppe to arrive. Coming out into the brilliant sunlight, the African blinked and shook his head.

'God, I never realized that it was so hot. Here, hold my jacket a moment.'

Making as if to take something from his shirt pocket, he pulled off his jacket and tossed it to Giuseppe.

'I'm not your bloody valet,' snarled the Italian.

But he reacted instinctively and grabbed the coat as it came towards him. He was still holding it with both hands when Moriba hit him. The blood from his broken nose gushed into his eyes, blinding him. Half-stunned, he staggered away, but the black giant pounced on him like an enraged tiger.

At the foot of the steps, Giuseppe's comrades were

53

beginning to grow impatient. They presumed that their intended victim might have been out or in the bath when Giuseppe arrived, hence the delay. But, on the other hand, it was just conceivable that something might have gone wrong.

The lower part of the Scala degli Spagni is a wide stairway, at the top of which is a broad landing. It is thronged with tourists, men and women selling souvenirs and postcards, and art students busily sketching one of the most famous views of the city. Above, the stairs fork into two narrower paths which are hidden to those in the street below by the crowds. The attention of the waiting men was attracted by the outbreak of some sort of uproar from the left-hand path. Men were shouting and women screaming, and soon people began to run away down the stairs as though they were fleeing from a deadly pestilence.

Then they saw Giuseppe. His face was caked with dried blood and his features were contorted with pain. He shuffled down the stairs towards them as though he were drugged, but what they could not immediately understand was the strange way that his arms hung loosely, like a puppet whose strings had been cut. One of the men ran up to him and clutched his shoulder. Giuseppe howled in agony.

'Moriba! He broke both my arms.'

Pinned to his shirt was a sheet of paper on which Moriba had scrawled a message. 'Next time, it will be his neck!'

One of the men led the crippled gangster into the car and drove him off to get medical attention. The others slowly climbed the steps and entered the Hassler to settle their account with Moriba.

At the reception desk, the duty clerk was sympathetic but unhelpful.

'Signor Moriba? You have just missed him. He checked out of here not more than ten minutes ago. I am sorry, but he did not leave a forwarding address.'

That night, Giuseppe did not beat up Emilia.

Pino Astoli listened with subdued fury to the description of the discomfiture of his minions. He was sitting in the sumptuously over-furnished lounge of his duplex apartment off the Corso. The fact that Moriba was a dangerous, cunning and violent man was well known to him. However, Astoli had the advantage that he was on his own home ground: he should be able to hunt down his prey wherever he might try to hide, whereas Moriba would be groping in the dark in an unknown city.

His reflections were disrupted by a piercing scream from one of the bedrooms. It was the voice of Monique, and Astoli leaped to his feet and rushed up the stairs.

His mistress was in hysterics. In her arms, she carried the body of a dead dog. It was the tiny toy poodle which had been her special pet and which haunted her bedroom and accompanied her everywhere. A piece of paper was pinned on to the corpse by a long needle. Astoli snatched the paper and read what was written on it. 'Next time, it will be HER neck!'

Pino Astoli was a realist. If Moriba could penetrate his home with impunity, he must already have allies in Rome. And while he was a man who could murder his enemies or, if it were to his advantage, his friends, he was genuinely fond of Monique and terrified that she might be hurt. He decided that he had to come to terms with Asi Moriba, at least for the time being.

It was the following day that Anna arrived at the Hassler and learned that Moriba had departed. However, when she gave her name, she was handed a note which had been left for her by a woman that morning. It gave her a phone number. She called from the hotel and was answered by Emilia who told her to come to a bar in Trastevere.

It was a dingy place; the walls, which had been varnished in the remote past, were adorned with a two year old calendar and some fly-blown posters advertising a number of horror movies which had long ago sunk into well-deserved obscurity. In a district which had become a fashionable focus of the artistic and more bohemian in-crowds, this down at heel dive survived as a reminder of a grim, poverty-stricken past, an aspect of the old Rome which had been conveniently obscured by all the razz-matazz of La Dolce Vita.

A bleary-eyed man behind the bar reluctantly offered to serve her while Anna looked around. There was no sign of Moriba. At one table, a group of men in shirt sleeves, possibly truck drivers, were playing cards and helping themselves to slices of ham and sausage and glasses of red wine. Anna's appearance did not seem to excite their curiosity and, after a casual glance in her direction, they went on with their game. She took a glass of Punt e Mes which the barman had poured from a bottle which was covered by a layer of dust thick enough to do justice to a vintage port, and settled down to wait.

Since she was watching the entrance, she did not notice the arrival of Emilia, who had secreted herself in the back kitchen while she kept Anna under observation.

'It is you who have been summoned by the big black man?'

Anna stared in astonishment. What on earth was Asi Moriba, a man of impeccable, if at times very kinky, taste doing with some faded and badly battered streetwalker?

Emilia must have guessed what was going through her mind, for she bristled defensively.

'Your man has got into a very dangerous spot and I am

the only person in the whole of this city who has done anything to help him. I have taken big risks myself, so you might as well trust me.'

'Where is Moriba?' Anna demanded.

'He is in hiding, not far from here, and I shall lead you to him. But I had to see you first to warn you to be careful. A slip on your part could give away where he is lying low.'

Emilia proceeded to give Anna an account of Moriba's encounters with Giuseppe and Astoli and then, after making sure that they were not being followed, led the way through the winding streets to an unassuming, two-storeyed house.

Inside, she found that an old, traditional dwelling had been converted into a modern, comfortable home. Even while he had been in Salamba, Moriba had invested in real estate throughout the world, and some of these buildings had always been regarded by him as possible refuges in case it became necessary to get out of his African homeland in a hurry. He greeted her without any great show of affection.

'Does she have to stay?' Anna asked, turning a hostile glance at Emilia.

'Why not?' Moriba replied. 'She is our eyes and ears in this city.'

'There are some things which are better done by the two of us on our own,' Anna pointed out.

Moriba laughed. 'No need to be shy. Emilia has seen it all in her time.'

Anna frowned. She did not object to playing any sex game in front of Emilia, or anybody else who might care to be a voyeur or a participant. But persuading Moriba to surrender the Golden Phallus, the obsession which had lured her out of Ibari, was an activity which could be hindered by the presence of this interloper. Her problem

57

was solved by Emilia herself who announced that she had better be getting back to her own place. If any of Giuseppe's friends noticed that she was absent for too long a time, they might become suspicious.

'I'll phone you if there is anything to report,' she told Moriba. 'Otherwise, I shall try to come by tomorrow.'

She kissed him lightly on the cheek, nodded an unconcerned farewell to Anna, and let herself out.

The afternoon was passed in gossip, and Anna's detailed account of what had been happening in Salamba since Moriba's flight. Then he outlined his plans for gaining control of the white slave trade, and the part which she could play in the operation, together with his intentions of laying his hands on every other remunerative racket in Rome. But at dusk, Anna got down to the serious business of seduction, and she found that her host was in a responsive mood. Moriba had always been a lusty performer, and his fall from power in Salamba had done nothing to diminish his appetite.

Anna knew from sore experience that the man was a macho monster, absolutely devoid of any trace of gentleness or consideration towards women. She had taken the initiative by joining him on a sofa and letting her fingers run over his cheeks before kissing him on the lips. It seemed that this slightest of provocations acted as a trigger to volcanic, pent-up forces within Moriba which he had been repressing, awaiting her arrival and their reunion.

He grabbed her savagely by the wrist and pulled her into the bedroom. Without a word, he literally ripped the clothes off her and flung her onto the bed. Pulling off his own pants, he proudly displayed his huge erection before her, then roughly thrust her head down and forced her to take him in her mouth. She ran her tongue playfully the length of the heavily veined shaft, but the vigour with which he drove into her wide, gaping mouth gave her no opportunity for finesse.

But this part of her ordeal did not last long. He pulled himself free, and for a moment she saw his wildly rolling eyes and tightly clenched teeth between his half-opened lips, a crazed jungle cat with bared fangs, before she was hurled face down on the bed. Her legs were yanked apart and that rigid, relentless piston, soaked with her saliva, was plunging into the depths of her, as if he were striving to split her womb.

It hurt, but fortunately Anna lubricated quickly and she moved to his rhythm, rather as a skilled boxer might ride punches. He was gripping her breasts, pinching her nipples so hard that her eyes watered. She could hear his ragged breathing in her ears as the tempo mounted, and she felt that her ribs would crack under his weight, pressing down on her. Then, with a deep-throated roar, he shot his load in a mighty fountain within her. The tension passed from his limbs, and he let himself sag out of her onto the bed. He had nearly suffocated her, and she thankfully gulped lungfuls of air.

'It must have been quite a time since you enjoyed anything as good as that!' Moriba exulted.

Anna was not so foolish as to contradict him. Now that the first fury had passed, there should be some scope for her to bring him to a more tractable frame of mind. Although the Golden Phallus dominated her thoughts, Anna never mentioned the object. They watched the sun set over the imposing dome of St Peter's and then ate dinner in the house. Anna encouraged Moriba to drink copiously in the hope that this would slow him down somewhat. It was in a mellow and contented mood that Moriba retired to bed for the second time that evening.

'Don't go to sleep yet,' Anna called in alarm.

Moriba, already between the sheets, answered her with

a languid yawn. Anna kissed him fervently, and her tongue sought his with a wild urgency. At the same time, she gently massaged his balls and his soft, placid cock. Gradually, he began to respond to her, and it was with satisfaction that she felt the stirring of his body. She moved herself over him, and let her breasts float above him, rich, luscious fruit, until she slowly lowered them to his questing mouth. He sucked first one tit then the other, like a sated baby.

They were good – so firm and yet so satin smooth. Inevitably, inexorably, his penis began to take a renewed interest in the proceedings. Her own excitement was mounting and her glands were flooding love juices through her eager vagina, spilling down on to the tops of her thighs, easing the way for the entry of his now fully erect cock. She slid him into her and slowly snaked her way up and down. At first, he was prepared to lie practically inert and let her do all the work, but such was her insistent sensuality that he could not long resist her, and he began to play a more active part. She showered kisses over his neck and face, and nibbled his ears while she clutched his strong buttocks and imperceptibly accelerated the pace of their carnal dance.

'You do love me, don't you, Asi,' she implored.

'As much as I love anybody,' was the cynical reply. 'But don't try any of your woman's tricks on me. I know very well the way you have manipulated your lovers and I don't intend to become just one more victim.'

Anna did not reply, but concentrated with the work of driving her man to a higher pitch of frenzy. She sensed him approaching his climax, and she at once slowed down in order to tantalize him until he could barely stand the strain. His muscles were growing taut and his breathing ragged. Little grunts and moans punctuated his panting, and his limbs glistened with beads of sweat. As his fever mounted, he attempted to turn her onto her back, but she resisted. Poised over him, she had the psychological advantage: it was she who called the shots.

Anna judged her moment well. She knew from many observations that there is one brief, delirious pre-orgasmic instant when no man could deny her anything. Moriba was striving to drive upwards into the innermost depths of her, and his fingers were wildly kneading her flesh.

'Asi, you will give me the phallus, won't you,' she coaxed.

'The phallus? You have the only phallus that matters, right there firmly between your legs.' His voice was muzzy and thick.

'The Golden Phallus of Osiris, Asi. It really ought to be mine. Say that I can have it. Say it now.'

To add emphasis to her demand, she withdrew her tongue from him and began to withdraw her cunt.

The threat was effective: his surrender immediate.

'Sure, yes, anything you say. You can have the Golden Phallus. Now, come back.'

Satisfied at her triumph, Anna closed in on him. With swift, decisive thrusts she brought him to the orgasm for which he craved, and pumped him dry, before letting him relax, fulfilled and exhausted.

They were both tired and, after washing quickly, got ready to go to sleep. Moriba was on the point of turning out the light, when she stopped him.

'Let me see it first, Asi darling, only for a minute.'

'See what?'

'The Golden Phallus. You did promise it to me, but we can share it.'

He roared with laughter. 'Of course you can have it. But first you will have to find it. I haven't got the damned thing: I thought that it was still in Salamba and that by now it would be in the greedy little hands of Milos.'

She started in alarm, like a cat from whom a saucer of cream had suddenly been taken. But it was clear to her that he was telling the truth. She shook her head in bewilderment.

'How can it be? I know Milos doesn't have it and if you don't, where is it?'

'I don't know,' Moriba replied. 'And I don't care. Just think, woman, of all the money we can get from the rackets which I shall control in Rome, that is more wealth than you have ever dreamed of. So who is interested in some archaeological relic?'

'You don't understand,' she hissed. 'It's not simply what it is worth. The thing is sheer magic. I must have it.'

'Go to sleep,' Moriba told her. 'We can talk about it in the morning.'

However, something was soon to occur which revived the interest of Asi Moriba in the fragments of the golden statue of Osiris.

# 4

## A Goose Lays a Golden Egg

Sandra had been waiting anxiously for days for news from Salamba. When she and Donald had escaped, they had left their friends virtually besieged in a remote mining camp. By now, Milos's soldiers must have forced an entrance and they would have searched feverishly for the Golden Phallus which had been hidden there prior to Sandra's stealthy smuggling of the relic. Louis Halevy, perhaps the world's leading authority on the artefacts of ancient Egypt, had been in the camp, and naturally Milos would have assumed that he would be in possession of the phallus. Sandra dreaded to think what actions he might have taken when he found that the Frenchman did not have it.

This was on her mind while she half-heartedly went over the words of a new number which she was going to sing that evening. Donald had gone to a gymnasium for a work-out and she found it impossible to concentrate. The Golden Phallus itself lay concealed in her saxophone case. The two of them had decided not to deposit it in the hotel safe: they considered that the fewer people who knew of its whereabouts the better.

As if to reassure herself that it was safe, Sandra went into the bedroom and took the polished, golden rod from its hiding place. As always when she touched it, she felt a strange sensation as though the metal were alive. Unconsciously, she started to run her fingers along it and the tingling grew more intense.

Her mystic masturbation was interrupted by the phone ringing. It was Halevy, calling from Paris.

'I got back this morning,' he told her. 'My concierge gave me the number you left with him when you called. I realized that it was from you, of course. Is everything all right: what about our phallus?'

'I was rubbing it for luck when you came through,' she told him. 'Maybe it is a sort of sexual Aladdin's lamp and will bring you whatever your heart desires.'

'Quite the reverse,' Halevy contradicted. 'It does not satisfy lust; it seems to provoke it.'

'Never mind that, tell me about yourself. Are you OK? I was so worried. Did you have a bad time getting out?'

'I am unhurt. We were shoved into a filthy prison while Milos's men searched every inch of the camp and ransacked our possessions over and over again. I stuck to my story that the phallus had disappeared by the time I arrived. Eventually, I think they swallowed it and concluded that Moriba had grabbed it before he got out. I kept waving my French passport, and I am certain that it was fear of an international incident which persuaded them to let me out without subjecting me to torture of some kind.'

Sandra turned as she heard Donald's key in the door. She called to him that she was talking to Halevy.

'Now, you must get the Golden Phallus to me as soon as possible,' the Professor told her. 'Before long the jackals in Ibari, and maybe other more sinister types, will work out that it must have been either you or your boyfriend who took it, and then both of you will be in great danger if you still have it in your possession.'

Sandra agreed, and promised to call back with details of the first possible flight which she and Donald would take.

'Don't delay,' Halevy warned again. 'And we shall have a celebration such as you will only find in Paris. I have a surprise waiting for you, a friend of yours.'

'Who?'

'You will see when you get here.'

He hung up, and she related the conversation to Donald. He kissed her and pointed to the way she was still caressing the Golden Phallus.

'You know, just the sight of that thing turns me on. We don't have to wait until we get to Paris, darling; let's have our celebration now.'

He took her hand and led her into the bedroom.

A couple of months before the revolution in Salamba, a stormy interview had taken place in a government office in Cairo. The Minister of Tourism was venting his annoyance on the head of an unhappy contractor.

'Get rid of it,' he shouted. 'It is an eyesore and it obstructs the road into Thebes. I told you about it last year, and the year before, and what have you done? Absolutely nothing!'

The target of this diatribe was a sad-looking, overweight man of indeterminate age. He rolled his shifty, black eyes in silent entreaty, and nervously rubbed his hands together as if he could somehow wash away his responsibility.

'But, Minister,' the miserable wretch implored, 'what can I do? I am fully of your opinion that it is very ugly, but the statue is a historical monument. It cannot be destroyed.'

'Destroyed!' thundered the outraged statesman, 'Who said anything about destroying it? You are a fool!'

'Yes, effendi,' agreed the contractor.

'All you have to do is move it. Do you understand? Shift the bloody thing a hundred metres, so that it is out of the way.'

'But, your honour,' the contractor pleaded, 'the statue,

on its plinth, must weigh a hundred tons. How can we possibly move it?'

'That's your problem. But if that thing is not out of sight of the tourist buses within three months, you will never receive another contract from the government. Do you understand?'

The contractor nodded weakly.

'Now, get out!'

The contractor fled.

The object which had so excited the displeasure of the Minister was a grotesquely misshapen statue, which local guides claimed was of one of the later Roman emperors. It certainly did not fit in with the brooding, majestic monuments of ancient Egypt which the tourists visited in their millions, and standing as if it were a petrified hitch-hiker on the road to the Valley of the Kings, it had attracted a great deal of ribald comment. This would not have mattered but for the fact that the Minister of Tourism, who had gone along with the tradition of its antiquity, had been humiliated by a visiting American professor who declared the monstrosity to be a fake. To have admitted that would have been a blow for the picture postcard industry and would have offended curio shopkeepers. Hence the idea of putting it somewhere less conspicuous.

Three months later, the contractor had not succeeded in displacing the monument, but he had made some progress. After all, his forefathers had managed to have the pyramids erected by huge gangs of forced labour: they would have disposed of a mere stone pillar before lunch. He was somewhat less efficient. It was now well after lunch, and the offending chunk of masonry had been manoeuvred onto a low trolley which had been constructed for the purpose. Ropes had been attached to its head to steady it, as a huge squad of labourers inched it away from its former site. As a result of their efforts, the road was now completely blocked, and the driver of a tourist bus was howling threats and insults at everybody concerned with the operation.

Some of the passengers dismounted from the bus, since it was clear that the delay was going to last some time, and they strolled over to watch what was going on.

'Do you think that it's safe?' asked a young woman schoolteacher. 'It looks top-heavy.'

Her companion was a freelance journalist who had worked with papers in New York and a number of European countries.

'I guess they know what they are doing,' he replied. 'It's the head that's causing the trouble. I've never seen a statue which was so out of proportion. That head must be twice the size it ought to be.'

'It's hideous,' the woman said.

The statue was swaying ominously as the men heaved on the ropes, and the trolley groaned and creaked under the weight. The driver of the bus had attached himself to the foreman of the gang and was urging him to hurry his men along.

Perhaps because they were being pestered, the fellahin did try to move too fast, or maybe the trolley gave way under the strain. Whatever the reason, the statue teetered uncertainly, and then its tilt became uncontrollable. Restraining ropes snapped or were jerked out of the hands of the men, and with a rumble rather than a crash, the monument fell to the ground.

A dense cloud of dust arose and the earth shook with the force of the impact. The workmen waved their arms and shouted excitedly, the bus driver gazed, stupefied amid the confusion, at the debris, and the horrified contractor ran up to inspect the damage. Fortunately nobody had been standing in the way, but the statue would never be the same again. The shock had decapitated it, and the gross head of stone had been shattered into a thousand splinters.

'Holy cow, look at that!' breathed the journalist. 'Here, quick, let's get some pictures.'

He and the teacher were both carrying cameras and they busily took photographs. What had excited them and other onlookers was not the state of the hideous relic, but what had been concealed within the stone head. For now, lying on the ground, was another head, this time undoubtedly of an Egyptian god. It was an object of classical beauty; the high cheekbones, strong chin and finely chiselled nose had all been executed by a master craftsman. And, as far as they could make out, it was made of gold.

Of course, there was an enormous fuss. The contractor placed the head in a tent which he had been using on the site for storing tools, and ran to phone an official of the Ministry of Tourism, who in turn alerted the Department of Antiquities. Eventually, a Professor Khalid, of the National Museum in Cairo, arrived at the scene and examined the strange discovery.

By now it was late evening and the bus and its occupants had long since departed. The contractor watched as Khalid fingered the golden head.

'What is it, Professor? Is it valuable?'

Khalid frowned disapprovingly. 'Whatever it is worth is no concern of yours. All I will say is that it is a very fine piece of work, a true work of art, and is the most remarkable head of Osiris that I have ever seen. But it could have some much greater significance. There is one expert whose opinion I want to obtain, and that means getting to a phone. Meanwhile, it is important that adequate security arrangements are made. You will see to it that this relic is guarded, night and day. And I do not want the news of its discovery to be announced. It is vitally important that not a word of this must leak out until after it has been examined by a world-famous Egyptologist.'

So the head was removed to a hut which had a lock on the door, and a police guard was mounted on it. The contractor gave his oath that he would say nothing of the incident, but it was too late. The visiting journalist had filed his story, together with photographs, and the news was already out.

That night, Khalid put in a call to Paris, but there was no answer from the apartment of Professor Louis Halevy.

In the presidential palace at Ibari, Milos was in a foul mood. In dealing with government business, he had snapped at his ministers and their officials and cut short his meetings. He found it difficult to account for his bad temper. He certainly was not missing Anna. She was an imaginative and highly talented lover, but in recent weeks she had irritated instead of exciting him, and he had felt a secret relief when she took off to track down Moriba and the phallus. Not that Milos had lost his sex drive; the arrival of Isis had brought a new spice to his bedroom activities. Yet even the exotic priestess lacked something for which he inwardly yearned. More and more, he caught himself thinking of Sandra, recalling the way she walked, the sound of her voice or the pert impudence of her smile. It was ironic that the one woman whose presence he desired above all others was the one he had never possessed.

He was jerked back to reality by his private secretary tactfully reminding him that he was due at a meeting with Isis and her group to decide on what steps they should take to recover the lost Golden Phallus.

Halevy's warning to Sandra had come none too soon.

The assembled disciples of Isis in conference with Milos heard a report from police officials. It had not taken them long to trace the visit of Donald and Sandra to the mining camp, and the implication was obvious. While Milos had been concentrating on Halevy, and subsequently Moriba, the birds had flown the coop, carrying off their prize to London. A confidential message was sent to the Salamban Embassy, ordering the staff to discover without delay where the couple were staying.

'Do not worry,' Grunwald told Milos, with a confident smile. 'Once your diplomats give us their address, Isis will take over. Regrettably, there may have to be some violence, but we shall get the Golden Phallus back without anybody from Salamba being involved.'

Sudden panic seized Milos. He wheeled on the complacent banker.

'You don't hurt the girl! Do what you like to that pigmy boyfriend of hers, but she is not to be harmed.'

Grunwald and Isis stared at him, astonished at his vehemence, but Milos jabbed his finger into the Swiss man's stomach to ram home his point.

'We shall do whatever we consider necessary,' Grunwald bristled, as he indignantly brushed away Milos's hand.

Milos's face darkened, but before he could hurl out the threat which was on the tip of his tongue, Isis intervened with that quiet authority which she had acquired over both of them.

'Do not quarrel about something which will not happen,' she commanded. 'We have our way of persuading people without having to stoop to crude methods. I personally shall be responsible for contacting the girl, and you,' she said as she turned sharply on Grunwald, 'will do exactly what I tell you. Do you understand?'

Grunwald grovelled. 'Everything will be done in accordance with your wishes.'

Milos was silent. Although he could see that the woman was the boss of the Isis people, he could not suppress lingering doubts and fears.

'Can we now get on with the rest of our business?' Isis insisted frigidly.

Milos had committed himself to allowing the cult to found a temple in Salamba, which they claimed would become a shrine of lust, attracting men and women from all over the world. For the rest of the meeting, they hammered out practical details. In anticipation of Milos's assent and the recovery of the Golden Phallus, the followers of Isis had brought to Ibari some other fragments of the statue which their members had recovered over the years. At the end of their deliberations, Isis spoke to Milos.

'We should receive the information from your London embassy some time tomorrow. Tonight, Isis will demonstrate our gratitude to you for your hospitality.'

Milos nodded his acknowledgement and strode out of the conference room. Isis watched him closely and shook her head. She addressed her disciples.

'I did not appreciate how attached this president is to the Scottish girl. We must make sure that he does not lose his head and start acting irresponsibly. Getting the Golden Phallus is our only concern, and the weakness of Milos or anybody else will not be allowed to interfere. Tonight, the power of Isis will bring him back under our control. All of you will have your parts to play. See to it!'

That evening, the Feast of Isis took place in an enormous, candle-lit church, a building which had been designated a cathedral before Milos had overthrown the old regime, and which was now destined to become the Temple of

71

Lust. The imitation Gothic vaults had been draped with scarlet curtains, and the embrasures of the windows were covered by boldly coloured, erotic pictures. The pews had been removed, and the central nave was dominated by lines of chairs around three heavy trestle tables, on which had been piled dishes of food and sparkling crystal decanters of wine. A number of divans, on which satin cushions had been scattered, were standing in each bay of the side aisles. Standing on the high altar, and visible from every one of the divans, was a strange object, a headless, golden statue; the mutilated likeness of Osiris.

Milos, and the other members of his government who had been invited, were amazed at the splendour of the statue, but Isis, who formally received them, shook her head sadly.

'It has been the work of centuries to have tracked down the torso and the limbs of the god, without attracting the attention of those who do not share our faith. Yet all this will be meaningless, unless we find the two missing fragments. What you see is a work of art, but it is dead. Complete what has been already achieved, and Osiris will live once more. We need the head, to bring us wisdom, and we need the Golden Phallus to give us the lust from which life springs. That is the task to which we are called. And now the summons of the great god has been clearly heard by you too, Mr President.'

The first part of the evening was devoted to a conventional dinner. Native waiters served the guests and the hosts, and the meal was supplemented by some other plates which Isis assured them were dishes which would have been eaten by the priests and priestesses of Isis and Osiris, thousands of years ago. Isis herself took a silver platter and carried it to where Milos was seated.

'Eat, and partake of the abundance of the Land of the Nile,' she intoned.

Her voice was as soft and sweet as the tone of a rustic pipe, but her appearance was magnificent. She was once more arrayed in the splendid regalia which she had worn that night in Bali, and in her presence the awe and wonder of that bygone age inspired all those who were present.

The food which she offered was a strange blend of meat and fruit, the flesh of a kid which had been marinated with spices long lost to the modern world, and cooked with dates, figs and honey. Milos tasted it cautiously, but found it to be delicious. The wine also was something special, a vintage of so deep a red as to be practically black, and rich and heavy on the palate.

When the meal was completed, Milos was led to the divan nearest the altar, where he settled himself among the cushions. The other guests retired to the other divans, and only Isis and two of her acolytes remained standing. Solemnly, they took up positions before the headless statue reposing on the altar.

The air was fragrant with an incense which subtly combined the sweetness of summer flowers with the sharpness of rare spices, spikenard blended with lilac, sandalwood with briar roses, frankincense with dianthus. After the aromatic food and strong wine, Milos was drowsy. Through drooping eyelids, he watched Isis remove a papyrus scroll from her cedarwood box, which stood on a table close to the altar.

This time, her ritual was very different from what she had performed previously. Her chant was a lilting paean in which she was supported by her assistants, who joined in responses to her melodious phrases. And yet, there was a soothing, restful quality to the music which seemed to smooth out the wrinkles of care in Milos's brain and lay to rest all the worries which had perplexed him. He closed his heavy eyes.

He was fully awake, and his senses quickened. Before him, there stood the figure of Isis, entrancing and inviting. He wanted to get to his feet and cross to where she was waiting for him, but his legs were like lead and he was not capable of stirring. In helpless frustration, he gazed at the temptress whose smile mocked him and at the same time spurred him to renewed efforts to break his torpor.

Another woman, wearing only a scanty brassiere, panties and high-heeled shoes, had appeared and now joined Isis at the altar. To Milos's amazement and horror, he recognized Sandra. He wanted to cry out to her, to beg her to come to him and turn away from the sinister priestess, but he could not utter a word. Unbelievably, Sandra took Isis in her arms and pressed a kiss on her lips, while Milos writhed in invisible bondage.

The two women made love with a slow-motion deliberateness which tortured him. Sandra reclined on the altar, one arm embracing the golden statue, while Isis slowly pulled off her panties. For the first time, Milos was able to see the trim triangle of fine, golden pubic hair which he had often visualized and which he so wanted to touch. But it was Isis's hand that was on his beloved's Mount of Venus, and it was to Isis that Sandra turned that dazzling smile. With every caress his agony mounted, and he strained to free himself from his fetters and save Sandra from the snares of Isis.

But Sandra was obviously a willing victim. She spread wide her legs, and Milos could see for an instant the white flecks of her eager juices and her glistening pussy before Isis sank to her knees and thrust her tongue into that paradise, the centre of all his desires, the focus of his rising passion. Sandra twisted sinuously, as her body was permeated by the glow of pleasure which emanated from the masterful tongue of the priestess. Her eyes shone and she made little gasping noises, each of which racked

Milos. When Sandra clasped her legs around the head of Isis, he could feel the tenderness of that embrace and fury burned in his fevered brain.

He became aware of the presence of other participants in this rite of lust. Only he was lying on his own. On all the other divans, men and women were making love, sometimes in couples, often in threes or fours, and the church echoed to their shouts and screams of uncontrollable bliss. While they were being fulfilled, he was condemned to witness the woman he loved being served by another, and his balls ached and his penis stood as firm as a pillar of marble in helpless craving.

But now, Sandra's excitement was approaching its climax. She was calling out to Isis, begging her not to stop, to work faster and to press her tongue ever harder against her throbbing clitoris. Isis was gripping her, possessing her, loving her, devouring her and as, with a piercing scream, Sandra's whole body shook with the violence of her orgasm, something snapped inside Milos's skull.

He threw up his arms and found his tongue.

'Stop!' he shouted at the top of his voice. 'Sandra, come to me! Let her go, Isis, you bitch!'

He leaped to his feet and staggered across to the altar. Behind him, there was a confused clamour, as people disentangled their limbs and jumped off their divans. But Milos was oblivious to them. He was standing, baffled and mortified, confronting Isis and her two acolytes. Of Sandra, there was not a trace. When the truth dawned on his befuddled mind, he shook his head in anger, turned on his heel and, without a word, hurried out of the church, followed by the other guests.

The members of the sect clustered around Isis, questioning her and seeking reassurance. But her face was grim and her tone grave.

'This man's infatuation is far more serious than I had

thought, and the girl is a menace to us. We must find the phallus as soon as possible. If that had been here, he would never have been able to break free.'

The next day there was a tension in the air while everybody waited for the news from the Salamban Embassy in London. It was late in the afternoon when the answer arrived with the address of the hotel where Donald and Sandra were staying.

The Isis group were deciding on their tactics when Milos strode into the room.

'Before you rush off, you may care to consider the item I have marked,' he growled, and he slapped down on the table a rather tattered copy of a New York newspaper.

Isis picked up the paper and read aloud an account of the discovery of the marvellous golden head in Egypt. There was a stunned silence, and then Isis cried out in indignation.

'But this paper! It is five days old.'

'You are lucky to get it at all,' Milos retorted. 'Since the revolution, direct deliveries from the States have not yet been restored. That is a copy which has been sent to me personally from one of our overseas embassies.'

'It is the last piece.' Isis was ecstatic. 'Think what this means. Once we have this head and the phallus, the god, Osiris, will be restored. A new era will open.'

'First of all, you have to get hold of them,' Milos pointed out scornfully.

Plans had to be revised, and Milos left them to their deliberations. In conclusion, Isis gave them their orders.

'I shall go to London to deal with the girl and her footballer lover. I expect that the phallus will be with the man. Andrew Drummond, you are British, and will accompany me. Josef Grunwald will lead a party to Egypt. Cleo Janis and the rest of you will stay here to keep Milos under observation.'

# Part II

# 5

## *Cock-a-Hoop!*

'Just a minute, please, miss.'

The security officer at London's Heathrow airport tapped Sandra on the shoulder. Obediently, she and Donald stood to one side to let the crowd of travellers pass.

'Would you mind turning out your bag?' His tone was polite, insistent and suspicious.

With a sigh, Sandra emptied the contents of her shoulder-bag on to the counter. The officer poked about among her cosmetics, the wallet containing small change, French francs, passport and traveller's cheques, a couple of paperbacks, some holiday photos and a packet of birth-control pills. Judging by the expression on his face, he did not think much of her humble possessions. However, his features brightened when he unwrapped the tissue paper and lifted up the Golden Phallus.

'Hello, what's this then?' he demanded accusingly.

'Well, it certainly is not a dangerous drug or a plastic explosive, is it?' Sandra answered reasonably.

'I did not ask you what it isn't. I would appreciate a straight answer, young lady, if you please.'

Sandra stared coolly at the affronted representative of authority.

'I would rather not say,' she replied.

The security officer called over a senior official who wore a cap with a quantity of gold braid to distinguish him from his minions, and complained of Sandra's intransigence. The newcomer fingered the phallus gingerly.

'It's got a funny feel to it,' he pronounced. 'Sort of

makes you tingle, and not only where you are holding it. And it's so heavy, you would think that it was solid gold. But I can't see that it is dangerous.'

'You would if you were hit on the head with it,' interjected Donald, who was infuriated by their bumbling officialdom.

Both the officers stared at him as if he were a maggot which had crawled out of their salads. Exasperated, Sandra burst out, 'Very well, since you are so damned inquisitive, I'll tell you. It is a dildo.'

'A what?' enquired the junior inquisitor.

His colleague whispered something in his ear, and the officer blushed bright scarlet.

'Downright disgusting!' he pronounced. 'I think that we ought to seize it as an obscene object.'

'But we are taking it out of the country, not bringing it in,' Donald pointed out. 'If anybody has a right to object, it would be the French customs.'

'The French!' he exploded. 'We all know what a dirty-minded lot they are. We can't expect them to make a stand for common decency.'

'Before you say anything else which you may regret, I would inform you that this is a sample of a dildo designed to sweep overseas markets and earn vast sums of foreign currency for Great Britain. My collaborator,' Donald nodded gravely in the direction of Sandra, 'has already been nominated by the Prime Minister to receive the Queen's Award for Industry.'

'Jolly good!' The senior officer handed the phallus back to Sandra, and smiled his approval. 'That shows real imagination and initiative. Just what the country needs!'

'I still think that it is a scandal,' his puritanical assistant grumbled.

'You are a stupid, narrow-minded hypocrite,' his boss told him.

Sandra stuffed her possessions back into her shoulder-bag, and she and Donald proceeded on their way. The two security officers were still arguing fiercely as they passed out of earshot.

On their arrival at Paris, they passed through customs without any further difficulty, and they were greeted in the concourse by Halevy. He led them to his car, in which was waiting a tall, athletic-looking girl.

'Petra!' cried Sandra. 'What the hell are you doing here? I thought that you were still in Salamba.'

'I told you that I had a surprise for you,' said Halevy with a knowing grin. 'Petra did more than anybody to help your girlfriend break out of Moriba's prison,' he commented to Donald.

'I fought to get rid of Moriba,' Petra told Sandra, 'but after their glorious revolution, nothing had changed except the guy at the top, and Milos the dictator turned out to be a very different man from Milos the freedom fighter in the jungle. So, I quit.'

'And came back to Paris to study at the university with me.' Halevy smiled contentedly. 'She had been one of my students before she went to Africa and got caught up in the struggle in Salamba. I had become very fond of her and, although I said nothing at the time, I was dreadfully worried that she would get herself killed.'

'I think that the sense of danger helped to bring us closer together,' Petra said, and she lovingly squeezed Halevy's arm, as he drove off towards the city centre.

'How is our phallus?' Halevy asked. 'I hope that you have been treating it with the respect due to the sexual organ of a very illustrious god.'

By way of answer, Sandra withdrew the libidinous sceptre from her bag and handed it to Petra.

'That feels good,' Petra purred. 'I get a horniness in my pants simply from holding it.'

81

'You weren't exactly frigid before,' Halevy laughed.

They went back to Halevy's apartment and, after freshening up, dined at a nearby bistro, where their host was greeted like a prodigal son. The food was delicious, the wine delectable and the conversation animated. At the end of their meal, Halevy turned to his guests.

'I invite you to an evening at a night club or a disco. However, there is another possibility, although I don't know whether it would meet with your approval. It depends on what Sandra feels about me, and how Donald takes to Petra. And, it goes without saying, my dear,' he smiled at Petra, 'on whether you like the idea.'

'What is this mysterious treat?' Petra asked.

'There is a rather exclusive club, not far from here, of which I have been, up to now, a non-performing member. It is called, intriguingly, The Double Cross. Only couples are allowed entrance, and then on the condition that, once inside, they swap partners. What takes place subsequently leaves absolutely nothing to the imagination. Let me say, for my part, that I would find Miss Mitchell a most acceptable bed-mate, but I don't know how the idea appeals to the rest of you.'

'Couldn't we make it a foursome?' Sandra asked, eyeing hungrily Petra's fine, firm breasts.

'I am sure that would not be considered an infringement of the club's rules,' Halevy answered, his eyes twinkling. 'What about you, Donald?'

Donald looked doubtful. This was not the sort of thing which had been encouraged in his strict Presbyterian upbringing. He glanced enquiringly at Sandra, but she was obviously amused by his hesitancy, so he nodded assent.

'I guess that Sandra has already agreed,' Petra chuckled. 'And, as for me, you forget that I still have the Golden Phallus in my bag. I have had such an itch in my crotch ever since you gave it to me that I am sure that I could take on the three of you, and still come back for more.'

The Double Cross was housed in a dignified building in a quiet street behind the Champs-Elysées. Halevy rang a bell and a small grille slid open. The party was carefully scrutinized: then the door swung open and they entered a space which resembled a scaled-down version of a hotel lobby. Halevy identified himself at the desk. Donald had to be enrolled as a temporary member: they each signed a declaration that they were not undercover police agents, engaged in the business of prostitution or, to the best of their knowledge, carriers of AIDS. Then Halevy paid an astronomical admission fee, and the facilities of The Double Cross were at their disposal. However, before they left the lobby, they were each presented with a lapel badge, bearing the name of a famous fictitious or historical character.

'It is our custom,' the receptionist explained, 'to ensure that the rule of the club is observed. You come in pairs, and the names on your badges are of romantic couples. You, mademoiselle,' he said to Sandra, 'are Juliet, so your friend is Romeo. Once inside, you will be free to bestow your favours on any man or woman, except Romeo.'

'And what happens if we cheat?' Donald asked.

The receptionist frowned. 'But that, monsieur, is the purpose of the club. Here, everybody cheats.'

'What I meant,' Donald said patiently, 'is what happens if Romeo and Juliet are found together?'

'Then, you are fined. You have to pay for champagne for everybody who is in the club.'

'Don't do it,' Sandra laughed. 'I'm not worth it.'

The receptionist handed each of them a key. 'Go through the door on your left. You will find there

83

changing rooms where you can undress and leave anything of value. There is also, in each room, a garment
which you should wear to enter what we term the Games
Room, which is through that other door, on your right.
May I wish you an enjoyable evening's entertainment.'

When they emerged from the changing rooms, they
were wearing silk robes, similar to kimonos, to which
they had pinned their lapel badges. Romeo-Donald and
Juliet-Sandra were joined by Dante and Beatrice, and
together they went through the door into the Games
Room.

They found themselves in a roofed-in garden, full of
sweet-smelling flowers. On both sides, there was an
arcade of fluted columns, behind which was what
appeared to be a row of alcoves. As they approached,
they saw that these bowers were in fact luxuriously fitted
rooms, open to the garden. In some of them, couples
were making love, while in others, there were whole
groups. Many were still unoccupied, and the four of them
took over one. Looking around them, they saw that all
their desires had been carefully catered for. The floor
was littered with cushions, soft and inviting, and against
one wall stood a low table on which there were canapés
of caviare and foie gras, a basket of luscious fruit, plates
of petits fours and boxes of choice cigars and cigarettes.
There were bottles of cognac and fruit juices, and a
magnum of vintage champagne stood in an ice bucket.
The Double Cross was an expensive club, but the management believed in giving value for money. Soft music was
playing and erotic films were flickering on a large video
screen in one corner.

At the threshold, Romeo-Donald kissed Juliet-Sandra
lightly on the cheek.

'Goodbye,' he said, 'see you later.' And he took
Beatrice-Petra by the arm.

Sandra would have replied, but Dante-Halevy's lips were against hers, and he led her into the bower. They settled themselves on the cushions, and Halevy brought over something to eat and some drinks. Petra lay back, like a contented cat, and let Donald feed her with morsels of caviare. At the same time, she slipped her hand inside his kimono, and ran her fingers up his penis, which had already attained lift-off.

Meanwhile, Sandra was relaxing, her eyes half-shut as she sipped champagne. She had slipped off her shoes, and Dante, apparently unconcerned by Beatrice's shameless dallying with Romeo, was tenderly massaging her toes.

'Mmmmm, that's nice,' she crooned.

'Isn't this even better?' queried Halevy, and he took each toe in turn in his mouth and licked them lasciviously.

'Sensational!' she breathed. 'But shouldn't we be more sociable?'

Swivelling her body round on her pile of cushions, Sandra laid her head on Petra's thighs, and pulled the other girl closer. Petra opened her legs, and Sandra fluttered her tongue against her exposed clitoris, thick, fleshy and pink. With a sigh of rapture, Petra sank back and Donald took one of her majestic tits in his mouth. Her nipple was firm beneath his lapping tongue, and the girl twisted her supple body in delight. They worked on her remorselessly, giving her no chance to escape from their hands and mouths which rapidly drove her to a frenzied orgasm.

Petra lay still, getting her breath back, and Sandra turned towards Halevy.

'Did you feel left out of things?' she cooed sympathetically. 'Now it is your turn, my love.'

She was hot and eager, excited by the way she had aroused Petra. That had been mere seduction; with her man, it was a case of outright rape. Before he knew what was happening, she had pushed him onto his back and virtually impaled herself on his shapely, circumcised cock. She grasped his arms firmly, and when he struggled to rise, pushed him back on the cushions until he subsided, happily resigned to his fate.

Petra gazed at the couple with amused admiration, but suddenly found herself confronted by Donald's own swollen, throbbing penis, which she caressed, at first gently and then gradually faster and harder. It seemed to be growing with every stroke. She stopped, and then ran her finger lightly around the glans, while Donald feverishly thrust his tongue inside her mouth, exploring its hidden sweetness. Abruptly, he pulled himself out of her hand and with a firmness which would not be denied, sank the quivering shaft inside her drenched pussy. They clasped each other and rolled about on the cushions, eventually coming to rest, with Petra uppermost, as their bodies bumped into those of the other couple.

Their climax was a once in a lifetime fantasy. The two girls, astride their men, kissed each other, full on the lips, and this was the last turn of the screw which drove Donald and Halevy crazy. Both of them were driving with the fury of the possessed, and Petra and Sandra could not hold back any longer. To decide which of the four succumbed to an explosive orgasm first would have required a photo-finish. For a brief eternity, they clung together, fused in the crucible of lust into an indissoluble unity of flesh and passion. Then, the afterglow of utter satisfaction crept through their limbs, and they let themselves fall back limply among the cushions and take a much needed rest.

They were still lying back when the receptionist walked through the garden and entered their alcove. He was carrying a case of champagne which he presented to them, with the compliments of the management.

'That is very kind,' Halevy said in a puzzled voice, 'but what is it for?'

'It is your prize,' grinned the receptionist, 'for putting on the finest exhibition of the night – indeed the best we have witnessed for a very long time.'

He pointed to where a miniature TV camera was concealed behind a bowl of flowers, and delightedly recounted how every twist and turn they had made had been displayed on all the monitors in the club, to universal acclaim.

'But now,' he said, 'I shall leave you to conclude what you have commenced with such splendid enthusiasm. Your champagne will be waiting for you when you leave.'

And with a courteous bow, he withdrew.

'How do you feel?' Halevy asked his guests. 'If you are tired after your journey, we can go home now.'

'It would be a pity to disappoint our public, wouldn't it,' Donald answered, as he pulled Petra towards him and started to rub her neck and shoulders in long, sensuous movements.

Sandra also made plain to Halevy that she was far from exhausted by running her fingers through the bushy hair on his chest and nibbling encouragingly on his ears. If the session which followed was not so unrestrained as their prize-winning effort, it had a languorous charm of its own, and at the end, they were just as deeply moved. Even after that, they were able to pet and caress, until they realized that they were the last people in the club. Reluctantly, they decided to call it a day.

'You know,' Halevy reflected, 'I'm not really young any more, and I don't do anything to keep myself fit. It's different for Donald: as a professional footballer, he is in perfect physical condition. I am surprised, therefore, at my own powers of recuperation. It was as though I could have gone on all night.'

The others agreed, but it was Petra who volunteered an explanation.

'Do you think that this might possibly have had something to do with what happened to all four of us?' she asked, and she pulled out of a deep pocket in her kimono the Golden Phallus.

'Good God! You brought it in here!' Halevy exclaimed.

'Of course I did. You told me that I should guard it with my life, so I was not going to leave it in a changing room with a flimsy lock on the door in a club like this, was I.'

Meanwhile, Professor Khalid was vainly ringing Halevy's home.

# 6
## *Eager Beavers*


After Monique's hysterical outburst, Astoli wanted to arrange a meeting with Moriba, either to kill him or to make peace, but he had no idea where to find his elusive adversary. He considered the problem, and when he thought about Giuseppe with both of his arms broken, he decided that he ought to have a talk with Emilia, and sent one of his toughs to bring her to him.

The prostitute was pushed roughly into the room, and she gazed sullenly at Astoli. With a toss of his head, he dismissed her escort and waved to her to take a chair.

'Too bad about your boyfriend.' Astoli's voice oozed saccharine sympathy. 'You must be having a hard time. Tell me, are you short of money?'

He pulled out a wad of notes from his pocket and offered them to Emilia. She ignored them.

'What do you want?' she demanded.

'Only to help you,' Astoli protested.

'I can look after myself,' she replied.

'Can you?' Astoli was all concern. 'What do you think is likely to happen to you when Giuseppe has got over his injuries? Or even sooner, if he talks to his brothers?'

'Giuseppe won't harm me while I am capable of earning money for him.'

'Not even when he realizes that it was you who betrayed him to that black mobster?'

'Who says that I shopped him?' There was a tinge of fear behind Emilia's defiance.

'It had to be you,' Astoli smiled. 'You were in the

room, listening to everything that was said, when Giuseppe was given his orders. And now this Moriba knows exactly where to lay his hands on Monique. Who else would have given him that information if it were not you?'

Emilia shrugged her shoulders. 'How should I know?'

Astoli's smile broadened. 'Try to understand. I am not annoyed with you. Giuseppe was a stupid bully: sooner or later, he would get what was coming to him. And as for you, Emilia, I am quite fond of you, and I would be truly upset if anybody did spell out to Giuseppe what you had done and he set his brothers on to you. They use knives, I believe, first on the face and then on more sensitive parts of the body. I would like to help you, to protect you if necessary.'

'What do you want?' she repeated.

'Just to get a message to Moriba. It's obvious that you are in touch with him. When he first came to Rome, he approached me with a proposition and I turned him down. That was a mistake: I misjudged the man. Tell him that we can do business together. He needs my operation here. OK, I am ready to talk. Let's meet. You arrange that and you will never have to worry about Giuseppe or his family.'

'If I happen to run into him, I'll let him know,' Emilia answered cautiously. 'You never know who you may bump into in Rome, do you?'

'Good girl,' Astoli assented. 'I like a woman who can use her brains as well as her pussy. You should go far, Emilia, and remember that if you ever need a favour, you only have to call on me.'

A couple of hours later, Moriba called Astoli, and a meeting was arranged for the following morning.

On his way to the rendezvous, Astoli summoned the gorilla who had brought Emilia to him.

'Tonight, after I have finished with Moriba, see to it that Emilia meets with an accident, and make sure that it is a fatal one.'

Moriba had taken a room in a hotel for the confrontation with Astoli, and he decided to take Anna with him. To her chagrin, Anna had found that Moriba's energy was devoted to pursuing his duel with Pino Astoli for control of the Rome underworld, rather than falling in with her wish to track down the erotogenic Golden Phallus, but she agreed diffidently to go along.

Moriba watched Astoli enter the lobby and made sure that he was alone before joining him and leading him up to his room where Anna was waiting. From the wide-eyed admiration with which Astoli ogled her, it was evident that she had made a great impression on the gangland boss.

'Say, is this dame going to be part of our set-up?' he asked Moriba in a lecherous whisper.

Moriba nodded gravely. 'But that can't possibly interest you. I am reliably informed that you are completely faithful to Monique.'

'That's right,' assented Astoli, 'but any small-time jerk can be faithful to one woman. I can be faithful to Monique and to this doll too, at the same time.'

'You are talented,' Moriba said sagely. 'Now, can we get on with our business?'

Anna glared at her unsolicited admirer, sniffed contemptuously, and went over to an armchair in the opposite corner of the room. As the two men started their discussion, she idly switched on a radio, just in time to hear a news flash.

'Listen, Asi, listen!' she shouted.

Moriba was taken aback by her excited interruption, and went over to hear the announcement. One of the news agencies had picked up the report of the discovery of the Golden Head, and it was presented as one of those random, curious titbits of casual interest. But there was nothing casual about the way Anna reacted.

'Asi, this must be part of the same statue. Think what it would mean if we could get hold of it!'

'In Egypt, is it,' Moriba mused. 'Perhaps you have got something. I suppose the thing is worth a fortune.'

'Say, what's going on?' Astoli wanted to know.

Moriba ignored him. 'They have only just found this head, so now is the time to take it, before all the sophisticated precautions have been set up. Hit them now, and we catch them off their guard.'

'Oh, Asi, will you do it? Say you will, please!' Anna implored.

'Why not?' he grinned. 'As a matter of fact, it could turn out to be quite a stroke of fortune.' He turned back to the irritated Astoli. 'Do you have contacts in Egypt who could help us pull off a job?'

Astoli's eyes lit up. This was the opportunity he had been praying for.

'Sure. What a coincidence! My brother is in Cairo. I'll give him a call. When do you want to go?'

'We shall take the first available plane,' Moriba said. 'And you will be coming with us,' he added sweetly.

'Me? Why do you want me on the trip?'

'Because, my dear Pino, our partnership is too fresh and fragile a thing. How do I know what you would get up to if I were foolish enough to leave you alone here in Rome?'

'You don't trust me?' The gangster sounded hurt.

'That's right. You come with us.'

Pino Astoli burst out laughing. 'You are quite right. I would do the same if I were in your position. Now, excuse me. I shall go downstairs and phone my brother to make sure that everything is prepared for our arrival.'

He trotted out, a radiant smile on his malignant features.

'Why didn't he use the phone up here?' Anna asked.

'Perhaps he did not want us to hear the arrangements for our reception that he is making with this newly discovered brother of his. However, it is very convenient, since I can now use this phone to place some calls of my own. If he returns before I have finished, I am sure that I can rely on you to keep him occupied. He obviously finds you very attractive.' Moriba chuckled. 'And he used to be so fond of poor Monique.'

'First the phallus and now the head of Osiris.' Anna was breathless with excitement. 'I always knew, deep inside me, that I was destined to recover what was rightly mine.'

Moriba cast an enquiring glance at her.

'You must know that it was my father who discovered the phallus and carried it off from Egypt,' she explained. 'They were after him, and he was running away from them when he got to Salamba. They must have caught him. My mother heard that he was in South Africa, and then nothing. Later we learned that he was dead, but we never found out how he died. They did it in revenge for his stealing their holy relic.'

'They? Who are they?' Moriba asked.

'How do I know? I suppose there have always been some followers of the old religion of Isis and Osiris, a sort of secret sect. But they had nothing until my father found the phallus, so it must be mine. Of course, I shall share everything with you, Asi; only get me that head and the phallus, please, darling.'

'You're crazy,' Moriba told her, shaking his head. 'Now, keep quiet while I get everything laid on for our expedition, before our dear friend, Pino, comes back and tries to eavesdrop.'

93

Moriba got busy with the phone, but it was nearly an hour before Pino Astoli returned, his face wreathed in a seraphic smile and brimming over with high spirits and good humour.

'You have been a long time,' Anna said in an aggrieved voice.

'Forgive me,' Astoli begged. 'I hurried to get back to you, so that we would have a chance to get better acquainted.' His mouth twisted into a leer of ingratiating lewdness. 'There were a lot of things to get fixed, and the lines to Cairo were busy. But everything is swell and you don't have to worry about a thing. I've arranged every last detail – flight, hotel in Cairo, limousine – and my brother will be at the airport to meet us, with a few of his friends who will come in useful. So relax, man: the next scheduled flight from Rome does not leave for another five hours.'

'On the contrary,' Moriba replied curtly. 'We take off as soon as we get to the airport.'

Astoli looked puzzled.

'We are taking a private plane.'

'But you should not have bothered,' spluttered the disconcerted Astoli. 'And it will cost you a fortune! Cancel the plane and take the regular flight. I have paid for the tickets for all of us.'

'You can get a refund when you are back in Rome. Now let's get moving!' Moriba picked up a small case, into which he had hastily stuffed a few clothes and toilet things. Anna had also packed while they had been waiting for Astoli.

'But my brother, he won't be there,' Astoli wailed. 'Wait until I phone him to let him know the change of plan.'

'There's no time now,' Moriba insisted, and grabbing

94

the Italian by the shoulders, he firmly guided him out of the room. 'Give him a call when we get to Cairo.'

In Paris, Sunday morning was bright and sunny, and slowly the quartet returned to consciousness after their night out at The Double Cross. Donald and Sandra had seats on an evening flight back to London, but they were not in the mood for a day's sightseeing, so they agreed readily to Halevy's suggestion that they go out into the country for a picnic lunch. He and Petra bought freshly baked crusty bread, cold meats, cheese, fruit and wine, and in a short time they were on the road.

About ten minutes after they had left the apartment, Professor Khalid phoned from Cairo again.

Halevy drove out of the city and took the road to Fontainebleau. There was the usual crowd of visitors to the château, but he took a side road which led through the extensive forest which had once been a hunting park for the kings of France, and before long they had the place to themselves.

They stopped and walked to a clearing, where the tall pine trees threw a dappled shade across the thick emerald grass. The only sound was the busy hum of insects and an occasional bird call, and the air was heavy with the fragrance of fallen pine cones. They were so imbued with the perfect tranquillity of the spot that they hardly said a word as they spread a cloth and laid out their food.

'Tomorrow, it is back to work,' Halevy said regretfully.

'I have to start intensive training,' Donald responded. 'And Sandy is singing in some club, reeking of stale tobacco and fumes from the kitchen, to say nothing of the sweaty bodies.'

'Don't spoil things,' Petra objected. 'It is so wonderfully peaceful here, let's enjoy it while it lasts.'

'Quite right, my sweet,' Halevy smiled, and he kissed

her. 'Our friends will have to get to the airport before very long, so let's make the most of what time we have left.'

'Will you go back to The Double Cross tonight?' Sandra asked.

'No,' Halevy replied. 'That was something special. As far as I am concerned, there has to be a close understanding between couples who indulge in group sex.'

'And the four of us are bound together by the custody of the Golden Phallus,' Petra remarked jocularly. 'How is it that an inanimate object from the remote past can have such a strong influence over us?'

'I think that it's all in our own heads,' Donald said. 'Don't you agree, Sandy?'

Sandra shook her head. 'I honestly don't know. I feel something when that thing is about, and so do you, Donald. You are a professor, Louis.' She turned to Halevy. 'What do you think?'

'Sex and magic,' he smiled. 'Is it so surprising that there is a connection? After all, isn't sex a sort of magic?'

After their meal, they were drowsy with the summer heat, and there seemed to be only one obvious way to conclude their discussion. Unlike during the previous night, the reunited couples lay apart, Donald and Sandra making love, disregarding the kissing and cuddling, the stroking and petting, and finally the fucking of the Professor and his student.

'Louis, my love, give it to me, just once more,' Petra pleaded.

'It will have to be a quickie,' he told her. 'Airlines don't delay flights for the sake of fervent lovers.'

'Don't take any notice of them,' Sandra whispered in Donald's ear. 'You can make time stand still, my darling.'

It was so good, leisurely and relaxed, without any trace of self-consciousness or tension, simply delighting in what came naturally and the joy of discovering, as if for the first time, each other's body.

Donald kissed her eyes shut, as if he were soothing and comforting a restless child.

'Last night was lust. This is love,' he avowed.

The sweet passion of her kiss told him that she could read what he felt in his heart without any need for words. He gave himself absolutely to her, and as they came together, she was his, without any shadow of reserve; their bodies were one, and so for that fleeting moment were their minds. Their love had become something sublime, a holy fire which fused their limbs together, but went on smouldering, white hot, after they had moved apart. They had learned to find complete sexual fulfilment, without recourse to the Golden Phallus or any other artificial stimulant or magic amulet.

'Time to be moving,' Halevy announced.

At Charles de Gaulle airport, they said their farewells.

'I hope that you have enjoyed your taste of Paris,' said Halevy.

'Marvellous! It was an unforgettable experience,' Sandra replied. 'I never dreamed that professors of Egyptology were so exuberant.'

'Louis has a very physical approach to his subject,' Petra laughed.

'Take good care of that phallus, won't you, Louis,' Donald advised. 'If we ever want to go back to The Double Cross, it will be invaluable.'

'What you might call an honorary member of the club,' Halevy asserted.

Sandra and Donald passed through passport control and turned to wave goodbye. Petra waved back, and as they walked out of the airport building, she drank in the warm sunshine.

'It's such a lovely evening. Let's not go home yet,' she suggested.

They parked the car in the centre of the city, and strolled hand in hand along the tree-lined boulevards, idly looking in the windows of the closed shops and boutiques, and pausing to have a drink at a café before dining in a Vietnamese restaurant close to the Opéra.

Back in Halevy's empty apartment, his phone had been ringing incessantly.

After their meal, the couple went to a movie. Halevy dropped Petra at the students' hostel where she had her own room, and it was after midnight when he let himself into his apartment. The phone was ringing, but it stopped just as he was about to pick it up. He shook his head in annoyance but dismissed the incident from his mind with the thought that if there were anything of importance, the caller would phone again.

It was the following morning when Khalid was at last able to speak to him.

'I've been calling you night and day. Were you away for the weekend?' demanded the Egyptian.

'I was tied up,' Halevy answered evasively. 'An international gathering which I had to attend. What is it that is so pressing that you need to call me from Cairo?'

Briefly, Khalid related the circumstances of the discovery of the Golden Head.

'You must come here without delay and look at this thing,' he urged. 'I need your opinion. You see, there is a local legend about a wonderful golden statue of Osiris which was supposed to possess supernatural powers. Of course, I always considered it to be mere superstition, but now this extraordinary head, certainly of Osiris and undoubtedly ancient, turns up.'

'Have you let your colleagues in the Department of Antiquities know?'

'Not yet,' Khalid replied. 'If I made such a sensational announcement and it later turned out that I had made some sort of mistake, that would be the end of my career. That is why I first want your confirmation. The relic is being guarded at the spot where it was found until I give the order for it to be transported to Cairo. But, once in Cairo, it would be impossible to keep it a secret. When can you get here?'

'I shall have to reschedule some of my classes. The earliest would be this Thursday.'

'Very well, if you can't make it before,' Khalid assented reluctantly. 'There was a leak of the story in the press, but it only got a short notice, tucked away on an inside page. I don't suppose that anybody noticed it, so another couple of days should not matter.'

Khalid was mistaken. As he was speaking, Moriba's jet was touching down in Cairo. It taxied across to an area reserved for private flights, and the party was shepherded into the terminal building, where they were met by an official.

'Mr Moriba?' he queried. 'Some gentlemen are waiting for you in the VIP lounge.'

Throughout the flight, Astoli's brow had been clouded by a worried frown. Now, the sun burst through.

'Great!' he exclaimed. 'That'll be my brother and his little welcoming party! He must have checked with the airport and been told of our change of plans. But they really ought to have waited in the car,' he added, as if speaking more to himself than to the others.

'No doubt,' Moriba observed. 'Please tell our friends that we shall meet them outside,' he ordered the official.

Astoli was frisking about, hurrying them through immigration control, but Moriba took his time, as though he wanted to draw attention to them and make sure that they would be remembered. He took the pilot of the jet aside and ordered him to stand by for their return flight.

'Check yourself into a hotel,' he said. 'I'll leave a message at the airport control when we want to fly back.'

'It will be expensive to hold the plane,' the pilot warned.

'Do I look worried?' asked Moriba ironically.

'We probably won't be here for many days,' Astoli reassured him. 'Come along, I can't wait to introduce you to my brother.'

Two large black Mercedes were waiting outside the doorway from the VIP lounge. As they were walking past, at a nod from Moriba, a couple of burly men hustled the unsuspecting Astoli into the back seat of the first vehicle.

'Wait! What's this?' he shouted. 'This is not my brother.'

'No, it's mine!' grinned Moriba. 'Make sure that no messy remains turn up anywhere,' he instructed the driver of the car.

Astoli's howls of fear and protest faded as the limousine slid smoothly away from the pavement, and Moriba led Anna to the second car.

'What was all that about?' she asked.

'Wasn't it obvious?' Moriba was at his most sardonic. 'There are quite a few people in Egypt, and in a lot of other places too, who owe me a good turn for services which I rendered when I was in charge of the police in Salamba. So, instead of Astoli's hoods disposing of me when we arrived, I returned the compliment. And if a precious relic shortly disappears, the authorities will be certain to recollect the arrival in Egypt of a notorious criminal from Italy, who will have disappeared, presumably with his spoils. So, at one stroke, I have undisputed control of the late, lamented Pino's business in Rome,

100

and we have an obvious culprit for the theft of the Golden Head, if I decide to go on with that scheme.'

At the other end of the African continent, President Milos listened with amused tolerance to Isis, as she informed him that she and Andrew Drummond were flying to London, and that Josef Grunwald would be leading a task force to Egypt that day.

'I am sorry to disappoint you, but none of you will be leaving Salamba today, unless you intend to walk out.'

'Are you threatening to detain us?' Isis demanded incredulously.

'Not at all. I invite you to join me and the people of Salamba in celebrating the country's national holiday. Every year, this is a day when not only do the shops and the banks close, but so does the international airport and the railways. I am afraid that your departure will have to be put off until tomorrow.'

That night, the devotees of the cult of Isis were the guests of Milos at an impressive feast. After they had dined, they were taken out into a huge open space, in which had been erected a kraal-like structure with a thatched roof supported by a double row of wooden columns. Rows of chairs and scatter cushions faced outwards to the grassy arena, around which thousands of Salambans were standing or squatting, chattering excitedly or singing in a confused babble. The President's party entered the covered enclosure, and took their seats in the place of honour.

Although the sun had long since set, it was still quite light, and now great, flaring torches were lit and planted in the ground, throwing gigantic shadows among the tall trees which clustered round the space, like silent onlookers of an atavistic drama. From all sides, there came the monotonous, insistent throbbing of war drums, and there was an air of expectancy which was almost tangible.

Suddenly, a gaunt figure marched into the middle of the open space. He was tall, and his height was accentuated by his ornate head-dress of ostrich plumes, dyed a brilliant scarlet and turquoise. He wore very little else, but what he lacked in garments, he more than made up for in jewellery and other ornaments. It was as though all the timeless past of the country had been personified in this one majestic presence. In a throaty, resonant voice, he broke into a chant in an African language, of which the Europeans present understood not one word.

Milos had been rehearsed in what was taking place, and he translated for them.

'When the world was very young, the great god, Mtili, wandered through all the lands from the deep ocean in the south to the high mountains in the north, seeking the most fertile valleys to be a home for the bravest of men. When he got to Salamba he halted, for he saw that this was the destined place. Then he called on Ndana, his consort, the most beautiful of all the goddesses, to join him so that they could procreate the race. Salamban warriors should be as brave as lions and as fleet as gazelles, so Mtili became a lion and Ndana a gazelle, and on this spot they came together, and from their union sprang the Salamban people. This feast re-enacts the divine coupling and the birth of the nation.'

The incantation finished and perhaps a hundred men sprang to their feet and broke into a savage dance. They were imposing, each of them more than six feet tall, ebony black, and with muscles like coiled serpents. They wore a strange tawny ruff round their necks, which Milos said were parts of the manes of lions which each of the warriors had slain with his own spear and bare hands. Around their haunches, there hung short skirts, made of more of the lions' manes. They stamped their feet in a rhythm which smashed into the brains of Isis and her party, until it seemed that their blood was pounding through their veins in time with the dance.

Then there was a change of tempo, and the relentless beat gave way to a quicker, more urgent, tripping measure, and a party of young women whirled into the space. Their movements were jaunty, as if to challenge and provoke the men, and they displayed their naked breasts with unashamed pride. From their hips, there swayed full grass skirts, and in their hair they had bound wreaths of a scarlet, hibiscus-like flower. Although they too were tall and well built, there was a grace in their beckoning arms and sensuous bodies which made them irresistible.

Now both groups joined, and the speed was growing manic. The drums had become ear-splitting. Isis found that she had to grip the arms of her chair to prevent herself from being carried away into that human whirlpool. She sat transfixed, unable to tear her eyes away from the spectacle of primitive courtship.

At the moment when she was sure that it had to stop, there was a raucous blast of trumpets which had been fashioned from the horns of wild bulls. At this signal, the men tore off their skirts and confronted the spectators with their genitals, glistening with sweat, their penises defiantly erect, the lances of an advancing army threatening their foes. The girls stood stock still; then they slowly shook their hips in a seductive motion, and let their own skirts fall to the ground. The warriors dropped to their knees, and each woman planted a foot firmly on one man's shoulders, so that he was staring straight up into her dark, open pussy. With an animal roar, the men seized them, and with one voice, the girls screamed strange words.

'They are calling on the men to give them lion cubs,'

Milos told his guests, and his voice was hoarse with emotion. 'Even older than the worship of Osiris, we had our own magic in this land,' he said to Isis.

The priestess could not reply. Spellbound, she watched as the males hurled the women to the ground and fell on them with all the fierceness of lions. There was a strangled shout, and she saw Josef Grunwald leap to his feet. His eyes stared, wild and unseeing, and the veins of his head were standing out as if they were about to burst. He had torn open his trousers and was masturbating with such fury that he looked as though he were trying to rip his cock from his body. To her amazement, when she looked down, Isis found that she too was massaging her aching clitoris, and all around her men and women were joining in the Saturnalia. As the young men rolled on the ground in the throes of their orgasms, the proud figure of the priest whose invocation had started the ritual stalked back into the centre of the arena. In front of him, four warriors led a live gazelle.

'He is the lion, the god, Mtili,' gasped Milos.

It was unbearable. His supporters held the struggling animal, while the priest, head erect and intoning a barbaric chant, masturbated ferociously. His relentless hands seemed to grasp the genitals of everyone present. At the moment he reached his climax, he roared as if he were truly Mtili, the lion, and one of the warriors, with one swift gash, cut the throat of the gazelle. The beast emitted a cry, half bleat, half bellow, and its knees buckled beneath it. It was over. Gradually, the crowd dispersed, and Milos rose to his feet. His face wore a tormented look. He alone of the party had not found physical relief. The image of a blonde Scottish girl refused to be banished.

# 7

## Cat among the Pigeons

The Minister of Tourism was furious. He pounded his desk, scattering papers on to the floor.

'You are an incompetent idiot!' he shouted at the quaking contractor. 'I ordered you to shift the statue, not to dismantle it. Do you understand the seriousness of your bungling? You have destroyed a priceless treasure of venerable antiquity, a work of incomparable beauty, an irreplaceable part of our national heritage. Tourists came thousands of miles to see it. And now?' He paused for breath, jutted out his chin and pointed an accusing finger at the human jelly before him. 'Now, it has been reduced to a heap of dust and rubble.'

'It was an accident, Your Excellency,' the contractor sobbed despairingly.

'Accident?' roared the Minister. 'And I suppose that you expect the Ministry to pay you for this accident!'

The contractor's wailing grew more intense. The destruction of the statue had indeed been an accident, but not to be paid for his work was a catastrophe.

'But, Your Excellency, I have to pay my workmen. They will starve, their wives and daughters be driven to prostitution and my family reduced to begging in the streets. Be compassionate!'

But the Minister was adamant. 'Pay you for this devastation? Next time there is work to be done, I shall employ Jenghiz Khan or Attila the Hun: either of them would be a model conservationist, a protector of the environment, in comparison with you. Get out, and make sure that I never set eyes on you again.'

The crushed contractor shuffled out of the office, and he was still shedding vain tears when he reached the street. A man who had been waiting patiently sidled up to him.

'My friend' – he took the contractor by the arm – 'this is your lucky day. I know all about the little mishap you had with that frightful statue, but a foreign gentleman has a favour to ask of you. And it is worth a lot of money.'

Suitably reassured, the contractor allowed himself to be steered to a hotel, where Moriba was installed.

'All I want from you,' Moriba told him, 'is to know when the head of Osiris is being transported to Cairo, and if there is a police escort.'

Anna entered the room, and the contractor's eyes popped out at such a miraculous apparition. Moriba threw a bundle of bank notes at him, and his eyes protruded even further. Allah indeed was all-merciful.

'At the successful conclusion of our business, you will receive the other half of your fee,' Moriba said with a smile.

The grateful contractor dived for the phone, and passed his instructions to the foreman at the site where the Golden Head was being kept under lock and key.

Louis Halevy called Professor Khalid on the Wednesday to confirm that he would be arriving in Cairo the next day, and Khalid promised to bring the Golden Head for him to examine. He called the foreman and told him that he would be arriving to collect the relic.

'I shall take it in my own car to Cairo tomorrow. See to it that there is a police escort.'

Within ten minutes, the information had been relayed to Moriba. Anna was dismayed.

'There will be a convoy of police cars,' she complained.

106

'And once the head arrives in Cairo, it will be guarded as closely as a nun's virginity.'

Moriba snorted derisively. 'With a little money, almost anything can be arranged. But with a lot of money – '

He did not bother to finish the sentence, but busied himself on the phone.

Late on Thursday morning, Professor Khalid parked his green BMW in front of the wooden hut which housed the Golden Head. The strange object was wrapped in sacking, and a couple of husky building workers, staggering under its weight, loaded it into the car's spacious boot. One police car took up its station in front of the BMW, and another nosed in behind it. As the three vehicles moved off, the foreman called a number in Cairo and reported full details.

It happened on a desolate stretch of road which passed through the desert. It was mid-afternoon, and the sunshine was being reflected in a blinding heat haze from the shifting dunes of yellow sand. The leading police car was well ahead of the BMW when Khalid saw the girl.

She was standing at the roadside, her dress dishevelled and her face stained with dust. The car was pulled halfway off the road; its front wheels were lodged among some large rocks and one door had swung open. As Khalid approached, she tottered and fell to her knees. He braked, and leaped out of his car.

'What has happened? Are you hurt?' he cried.

He took her in his arms and led her back to the BMW. He could not help noticing how pretty she was, despite her apparent distress. As he reached the door, the second police car drove up, but then accelerated away into the distance. Khalid opened the front passenger door, and helped the girl onto the seat. Then he walked around to the other door, where he found himself face to face with a black giant, who must have come out of the girl's disabled car while Khalid had been preoccupied with her.

'In the back,' Moriba ordered.

Any hesitation Khalid may have felt was dispelled by the sight of the pistol in Moriba's hand. Anna was busy, wiping the dirt off her face and straightening up her clothes.

'What do you want?' Khalid asked.

His captors did not bother to answer. Moriba drove the BMW off the road and about five miles into the desert.

'There,' he said with a kindly smile. 'Even in this heat, you should be able to get back to the main road in less than a couple of hours, and I expect that you will be picked up before nightfall. Any driver is certain to stop. Now, out you go!'

The hapless Khalid was deposited in the desert, and Moriba drove off at top speed. As he started trudging back, Khalid could not help reflecting on how pretty the girl had been.

It was very late that night when he got back to Cairo, in the cab of a truck loaded with vegetables for the market. Halevy had been at his office, trying to find him, and had finally checked into a hotel, so that it was not until the next morning that the two men met, and Khalid was able to give Halevy an account of what had happened.

The Frenchman listened in grim silence until Khalid described his assailants.

'A superbly beautiful girl and an enormous black man,' he repeated bitterly. 'I have a fairly good idea of who they are. But, tell me, in view of what you were carrying, why in the world did you stop?'

'Egypt is a land of the desert,' Khalid explained. 'Here, everybody stops if they see someone in distress. If you leave somebody in the desert, he dies. It is the same in all other countries, where to abandon a stranded traveller is to sign his death warrant. And besides,' he added wistfully, 'she was very lovely.'

The archaeologists contacted the police and Khalid demanded an explanation from the driver of the second car.

'Well, sir,' the policeman said, 'when I saw that you had a young girl in your arms and you were leading her to your own car, I thought that it would be tactless of us to interfere. It happens all the time, and we make ourselves scarce. After all, if a professor of Egyptology wants a bit of fun, why should we spoil things?'

Khalid was obliged to accept the driver's word, although he had a strong suspicion that the man was being less than frank. This feeling would have been greatly strengthened if he had observed the occupants of both police cars counting out their share of the dollar bills which Moriba had so liberally dispensed.

Of course, a search was made for the stolen head, but by then the jet had taken off for Rome, carrying a crate which purported to contain a defective part of the control gear of a nuclear generating plant, manufactured in Italy, and which had to be repaired or replaced as rapidly as possible.

Halevy waited for a few days, in case the police came up with a lead. Neither the contractor nor his foreman had any idea of who could have been behind the outrage, and they were well rewarded for their profound ignorance. But the police persevered with their enquiries and, before long, they had a definite theory. A smartly dressed young superintendent, who had been put in charge of the case, received Halevy and Khalid.

'We now have an important clue,' he told them. 'We have been checking with the airports and we have learned that a notorious Italian gangster flew into Cairo, only a few days before the theft. He was accompanied by a couple who fit exactly the description of the two who staged the hold-up in the desert. The pair of them have since left Egypt, but of course, they were only the Italian's accomplices, mere pawns in the game. This criminal, whose name is Pino Astoli, I am reliably informed is still in Egypt, and I am confident that when we find him, we shall recover this rare relic. We shall, of course, make every effort, but I must say that, personally, I don't know whether this strange object merits all the fuss which you are making about it. The museums are stuffed full of bits of ancient statues; does one more fragment make all that much difference?'

Halevy returned that day to Paris, but not before a final meeting with Khalid, during which he told the Egyptian that he was almost certain that there existed an entire statue of Osiris, and promised that if any part of it ever got into his hands, it would be returned to Egypt where it rightly belonged. He said nothing about the Golden Phallus and the quest for it.

# 8

## Monkey Business

During the flight back from Paris, Donald spoke little and appeared to be preoccupied.

'What's on your mind?' Sandra asked him.

'I was thinking just how much I shall miss you, with you singing in London, while I shall be playing up in Glasgow.'

Sandra squeezed his hand. 'Cheer up, darling. London is not the other side of the world, and I am sure that we shall find plenty of chances to get together.'

Donald regarded her in silence for a while.

'Why don't we get married?' Donald urged, his voice husky with emotion.

'Now, we went over that before we left for Salamba, didn't we,' Sandra replied in a gentle voice. 'Both of us are just starting on our careers, and I am no more prepared to be the docile wife of a professional footballer, traipsing round after you every time Rangers have an away match, than you would follow me from gig to gig. So, you have to be based in Glasgow, but I need to be in London, close to the big recording companies and the impresarios and managers, if I am ever to make the big time. Be reasonable, darling, we have plenty of time ahead of us, and I am very happy, going steady with you.'

Donald looked miserable and then asked, 'You do really love me, don't you, Sandy?'

'You know I do. What's got into you? It's not like you to be so insecure.'

'I don't know. Maybe it was seeing the way you made love to Louis Halevy.'

Sandra shook her head impatiently. 'Look, Donald, my dearest, get this straight. I love you: I want to go on living with you, although I am aware that we cannot be together every day and every night. I want to settle down with you in a home of our own and to have your child, but not yet. We are too ambitious to quit so soon. You have to play more internationals for Scotland, and I am not content with only having sung in a few clubs around Glasgow. And as for my swinging with Halevy, my body is my own to do what I like with. I am a free woman, and that's the way it's going to stay. Anyway, I didn't notice that you were so shy when you were eating Petra: I thought that you were going to call for mango chutney.'

'That was different,' Donald protested.

'Why? Just because you are a man? Christ, I believe that you are jealous, my poor, wee laddie.'

She was laughing, but Donald remained serious.

'I can't help it. I have a feeling that something is hanging over us, some sort of menace.'

'Nonsense. Now that we have got rid of the Golden Phallus, we have nothing to worry about. You simply haven't got over the traumatic time we had in Salamba. Come on, Donald, snap out of it!'

By the time they had got back to their hotel in London, Donald's gloom had lifted somewhat, but Sandra sensed that he was still ill at ease.

'Our last night together,' he complained, as they climbed into bed.

'Then let's make the most of it,' Sandra retorted. 'Don't be so dramatic: we shall be four hundred miles apart, one hour by plane and one minute by phone.'

She pulled him to her, ruffled his hair and kissed him repeatedly until he began to respond.

'That's more like my old Donald,' she grinned.

'I suppose that you are right,' he conceded.

'You know, you have divine hairs on your chest, all crisp and curly and crinkly,' she told him, and she twiddled and twirled them between her fingers. 'Just you make sure that you keep them for me. Don't you ever let anybody talk you into shaving them.'

'Now who is being possessive?' Donald taunted.

'You talk too much. Don't waste time,' Sandra riposted.

She was not able to say more because Donald glued his mouth to hers and forced his tongue deep inside. Her arms tightened around his shoulders and she rubbed her body against his, like a contented cat. Her happy sigh, when Donald came up for air, was a veritable purr. His hand was between her thighs, and he began to move his body over hers.

'No, not yet,' she murmured. 'Give me your tongue first; I love that.'

Obediently, he worked his way down, taking his time as he lingered to suck on each of her tits and to nuzzle in the tiny goblet of her navel. She arched her back, and pushed forward her eager clitoris to meet and greet him. His hands closed round her buttocks; full yet firm and beautifully rounded, they never failed to excite his lust. As he paid tribute to her with his hands and his mouth, a wonderful, sensual glow filled her, and her hands played with his hair and his ears. He was licking in long, slow, seductive sweeps across her vagina and clit, and then suddenly his tongue was a fluttering butterfly, barely brushing them, teasing and tantalizing, until she was ready to explode. But he was not willing to give her that relief yet. Instead, he withdrew his tongue and, deftly turning her over, let it penetrate her sweet arse. It added a new dimension to her ecstasy.

He revelled in her fragrance, her own scent which belonged to her and to nobody else in the whole wide world, and he felt that there was no other man or woman who knew her as he did, not merely the pretty girl who could attract swarms of lovers and admirers, but the real woman beneath the surface charm. It was this consciousness which made him so responsive to her sexual demands and such a considerate and pleasing lover.

'You can keep doing that for ever,' she mused dreamily.

But he didn't. She was basking in a drowsy torpor into which his soothing caresses had lulled her. As he transferred his attentions back to her pussy, a new tension ran through all her muscles, and she pressed his head closer as though she feared to lose him for even a fraction of a second. She was spurring him on to greater exertions, and his tongue ached under the pressure, but his own agitation made him impervious to any discomfort. He knew that marvellous, giddy instant when she completely lost control of herself, the moment of no return. She came with a hoarse scream, and her throbbing set fire racing through his veins.

However, he had to wait for his turn, for she pushed him away from her until she had got over that sensitiveness which she always experienced for a minute or two after such an orgasm.

'Mmmm. I guess I have the Golden Clitoris,' she gloated.

She lay on her back, and he mounted her with the smooth ease which comes when a couple are perfectly in tune with each other. Her eyes were shut and there was a smile of pure bliss on her lips. But she did not long remain a passive partner, and before Donald attained his own incandescent climax, it was she who was drawing him deeper inside her, and had claimed his penis as her own.

Maybe because they were both conscious of the nearness of their moment of parting, their sex was heavily charged with emotion that night, and they lay longer than usual in each other's arms, without speaking but savouring the happiness of being together, before drifting off to sleep.

In the morning, they packed and checked out of the hotel. Sandra had found herself a furnished flat a day or two before their trip to Paris, and now she moved in. It was a modest, but comfortable, studio in a quiet side street off the Fulham Road. It gave her pleasure to show the place to Donald, somewhere of her own where she could welcome him whenever he got the chance to make a lightning trip to London. Although the apartment and the tiny patch of garden outside, as well as all the furniture, belonged to somebody else, it would still be a home for them which no hotel room, no matter how luxurious, would ever be. They felt their way around, growing accustomed to the place, and went for a walk to find the local shops and the nearest Tube station. Back in the studio, Sandra brewed up a pot of tea.

'I suppose you will have to leave soon to get to the airport,' she said.

'I have a few minutes. Now, do you have my address and phone number?' Donald asked.

Sandra nodded. He had arranged to stay, at least temporarily, with his brother who had a large house in the Kelvingrove district.

'He's a vet, isn't he, your brother?' Sandra asked, as she poured the tea.

'Alec would prefer to be called a veterinary surgeon,' Donald informed her with a smile.

'What's he like?'

'Alec? Well to start with, he is ten years older than me, and a much more dignified gentleman. Kelvingrove

115

is a very genteel district, you know.' There was a faintly mocking air in the way he cocked his head as he spoke. 'But he's nice enough once you get to know him. Alec is the one with the brains in the family. He got a Highlands and Islands scholarship to the university, and did very well.'

'Glasgow?'

'No,' Donald laughed, 'St Andrews, a much grander place. But you'll meet him when you come up to Glasgow. Now that's quite enough about him. We have hardly any time left, so don't you think that we should try out your bed?'

'Donald McFee, I do declare that you are a demented sex maniac,' Sandra protested. 'You made a big deal in the hotel of celebrating our last night together.'

'Ay, well, now we should celebrate our last day,' he chuckled.

And they did, with the result that Donald came within a minute or two of missing his plane.

'Have you noticed,' Sandra asked as she put her clothes back on, 'that we seem to manage just as well without the Golden Phallus as when it was in the room with us?'

'I think that its mysterious influence was a lot of superstitious nonsense,' Donald affirmed. 'It all went on in our heads. I am glad that we are rid of the damned thing and that it will soon be stuck away safely in a museum where it belongs.'

There were other people who had very different plans for the relic. The woman called Isis and Dr Andrew Drummond had caught the first available flight from Ibari to London, and the two of them took a taxi to the hotel where they had been told that Donald and Sandra were staying. Drummond asked for Donald at the reception

116

desk, only to be told that he had checked out the day before.

'Did he leave any forwarding address?' Drummond asked. 'I have a present for Mr McFee.'

The clerk shook his head. 'Sorry, but no,' he said.

'What about the girl?' Isis intervened. 'Have they gone together?'

'I really cannot say,' replied the clerk indignantly. 'It is not our practice to pry into the personal lives of our guests.'

Isis snorted, and turned away in disgust.

'Have you no idea how we may be able to get in touch with Mr McFee? It is quite important,' Drummond pleaded.

With the air of one spelling out some elementary principle to an obtuse child, the clerk suggested, 'Why don't you contact his club?'

'His club?' echoed Drummond, puzzled. It seemed unlikely that Donald McFee would be a member of the Senior Carlton or Boodles.

'Glasgow Rangers,' the clerk explained. 'You must know that Mr McFee plays for them. He's famous!'

'Of course,' Drummond agreed heartily. 'It had slipped my mind. Silly of me.'

The clerk shook his head in disbelief. How could anybody forget which club a Scottish international played for? However, when Drummond passed him a five pound note, any doubts or suspicions he might have been harbouring evaporated.

It was getting late, so they took the night sleeper from Euston to get into Glasgow in time for breakfast the next morning, and during the journey they decided on their next step.

'I wonder if the girl is with him,' Isis said.

'It does not matter,' Drummond replied. 'You can be

sure that he would not give anything with the sexual power of the Golden Phallus to his girlfriend. No, find McFee, and we find the phallus.'

'As long as he hasn't put it into a bank or a safe deposit,' Isis objected.

'No. It is clear that this footballer knows nothing about Egyptology, nor is he a common thief. He happened to stumble on the magic property of the phallus, so you can be sure that he will keep it with him and take advantage of it. Why should he stuff it into a vault, where he would not be able to use it whenever he got the chance to make a pass at some pretty girl?'

In Glasgow, they found themselves a hotel and set about making their enquiries. They also sent for reinforcements, and were shortly joined by two hefty recruits who would come in handy in a fight, one of whom was an accomplished burglar.

Donald found that it required an effort to get back into the strict routine of training, despite the strenuous exercise he had become accustomed to take in bed with Sandra. On the field, quite different muscles were brought into play, and he limped off the turf, already frozen hard by early frosts, sore, stiff and sweaty. The vast stadium of Ibrox Park, with its tier upon tier of empty seats, was cold and forbidding after the cosy intimacy of Sandra's Fulham studio. But Donald was a highly talented footballer, dedicated to his chosen career, and conscious that in a few weeks' time those stands would be packed by cheering and shouting fans, who would expect him to produce dazzling displays of agility and control, so he grimly persevered in regaining his top form.

At the end of one of those gruelling training sessions, as he trotted off the field, Jamie McCann, the team's trainer, called him over. Standing beside McCann was a tall, distinguished-looking man, wearing an elegant grey suit which must have been made to measure by one of London's most fashionable and most discreet tailors. Andrew Drummond looked intently at his quarry, while McCann repeated to Donald his story.

'Donald, laddie, this gentleman is a very well-known medical man. He tells me that a group of doctors are making a study on cramp among athletes and sportsmen.'

'Cramp?' Donald queried.

'Yes, I know it may sound strange, but it is a serious matter.' Drummond spoke with all the authority of a Harley Street consultant, whose every word cost moguls, tycoons or royalty more than they spent on their mistresses in a month. 'For ordinary folk, cramp can be horribly painful, but as it is not a disease which requires attention, it tends to be ignored. However, because it strikes without warning, it can be serious, even fatal. Every year, some unfortunate swimmers succumb to an attack when they are in deep water, and we have reason to believe that a sudden spasm affecting a driver may be the cause of a number of traffic accidents, and the same probably applies to some industrial mishaps, often with grave consequences.'

'Very interesting,' said Donald, who was beginning to shiver. 'But what has that to do with me?'

'My dear chap . . .' Andrew Drummond sounded concerned. 'You will catch a chill. Let's go into the changing-rooms where I can explain, while you have a hot shower and get into some warm clothes.'

McCann led the way through the tunnel, and Drummond noted carefully the layout of the corridors and changing-rooms beneath the stands. He waited while Donald showered quickly. The footballer emerged, swathed in a towel, and the three of them walked into the locker-room. Drummond surreptitiously peered inside when Donald opened his locker to take out his clothes, but he could only catch a fleeting glimpse. Then he told them that since men and women who played games had learned to deal with cramp, the panel of doctors was examining a number of leading sportsmen and women, and interviewing trainers and coaches, in the hope that they would be able to formulate some simple system of prevention for ordinary people. Drummond next proceeded to question McCann on how trainers dealt with sudden attacks of cramp on the field, and carefully examined Donald, making copious notes in a leather-bound notebook. When he had finished, he thanked them both for their co-operation, and found his way out of Ibrox Park to where his two heavies were waiting for him in the car.

'So what was all that about?' Donald asked McCann.

'Just some harmless Sassenach,' McCann grinned. 'These snooty doctors have plenty of influential friends, so it seemed to be canny to humour him. Now, away home with you, man, and let's be seeing something of your pace tomorrow.'

Back in their hotel, Drummond reported back to Isis.

'I was only able to get a brief glance into McFee's locker and I did not see anything there.'

'Can you be certain that it is not in the locker?' Isis insisted.

'Not absolutely,' Drummond answered.

'Then we go ahead, as planned.'

Drummond drew a rough plan of the underground corridors at Ibrox Park, and pointed out to the ex-burglar the exact location of Donald's locker.

That night the two toughs broke into the ground and vandalized some of the changing-rooms to give the impression that it was the work of hooligans. Among other lockers, they forced open Donald's, but they found no trace of the Golden Phallus.

'So he must have it at home with him. It is what always seemed most likely,' Drummond stated.

Isis agreed. 'We have had a stroke of luck. There was a short article on McFee in one of the local newspapers which I happened to see. It appears that he is living with his brother, a vet. We can find his address easily enough from the phone directory.'

Alec McFee lived in the ground floor of the dignified Victorian mansion built in that rather drab brown stone typical of the Kelvingrove district. He had let the two upper floors, for the purchase of the house had badly strained his finances. Donald was sleeping in a small back bedroom from which his brother had removed veterinary and medical supplies which were now piled untidily in the front parlour, which doubled as Alec's consulting-room. A methodical man, Alec systematically kept drugs and equipment packed in a bag, which stood by his desk during the hours he was available for consultation at home. As soon as he closed his surgery, he placed the bag in his car so that it was ready if he were called out in an emergency or to visit a farm.

On Saturday, Alec had lent his car to Donald who drove to the village, about twenty miles away, where his mother still lived. Before leaving, Donald had handed the bag back to Alec.

'It's better that you keep this here,' he said. 'Some young kids might think it contains drugs and break into the car to steal it.'

His departure was reported to Isis by one of her toughs who were taking turns to watch the house. In the early evening, she was told that Donald had returned. She turned to Drummond.

'OK, Andrew, this is it. Let's go.'

Donald was sitting in the parlour when the phone rang.

'Damnation!' Alec cursed in his well-bred, St Andrews manner. 'That was a call from somebody out on the Cathcart Road. They have a golden retriever which sounds as if it is having a fit. I must get out there without delay and make sure that it is not a case of rabies. I'll be back as soon as I can. Make yourself some tea; you'll find some scones in the larder.'

He bustled out, and Donald heard him drive off. He had barely left the house when there was a ring at the front door bell. Standing outside was a breathtakingly beautiful woman.

'Mr McFee?' she asked, when he opened the door.

'Yes, but you probably want my brother.'

Isis smiled. 'No, Mr McFee, we have come a long way specially to meet you. From Salamba, in fact.'

Donald stiffened, but before he could close the door, the two members of Isis's heavy squad materialized from behind some shrubs and pushed him inside. He staggered back, and found that in addition to the two aggressive intruders both Isis and Andrew Drummond had followed him into the house.

'What the hell do you want?' Donald flared up.

'I think you know,' Isis said softly. 'We don't want to harm you, but you have something which belongs to us. Hand over the Golden Phallus nice and peacefully, and you will have no trouble.'

'The only phallus I have is the one between my legs,' Donald retorted.

Isis sighed. 'You are stubborn, but it won't do you any good.' She nodded at the two toughs, who started to search the house, rummaging through Alec's supplies which they spilled out of their cartons, breaking some phials and scattering pills and powders over the floor.

Donald leaped to his feet, but one of the men punched him in the stomach, and he collapsed, winded.

'Do be sensible,' Drummond told him, as though he were a mischievous schoolboy.

They bundled him into a chair, and while one of the toughs held him, Drummond produced a hypodermic, rolled up one of his sleeves, and with one rapid jab injected a fluid into a vein.

'That should make you more docile,' he smiled.

It stung, and he experienced a strange, cold sensation in his arm, as though there were a trickle of ice in his blood. He glared at Drummond in helpless fury, and then the world started to float about him. His brain was turning to cotton wool, and his head was too heavy for him to be able to keep it erect. He could hear Drummond speaking, his voice distorted, from miles away.

'He's gone under nicely. You should be able to get what you want from him now.'

Drummond disappeared, and in front of Donald there now stood Isis. He found it impossible to focus properly. At one moment, the woman appeared to be a tiny doll, far away and indistinct, and at the next she loomed up through the fog in his brain and seemed to envelop him. She was saying something to Drummond and Donald was able to hear his reply.

'No, it is not a truth drug. Indeed, there is no such thing as a drug which compels a subject to tell the truth, but what it does do is to greatly reduce his will power. He may possibly lie to you, but with your peculiar powers of persuasion, he will not be able to offer any resistance to you. Now, you had better get busy before his brother discovers that his emergency call was a hoax. That stuff is strong, but its effect does not last long.'

'It does not seem that there's anything here,' he heard one of the men who were ransacking the place call out.

'Now, my obstinate young friend, will you please give me the Golden Phallus.' Isis's voice was still good tempered, but beneath the surface there was an iron willed insistence.

He tried to shake his head but it was too much of an effort. A distant, strange voice said, 'No, I won't,' and he was amazed to realize that it was his own.

The miniature figure of the woman had a box in her hands from which she extracted a scrap of what appeared to be parchment. In a lilting, sing-song voice, she began a weird incantation which filtered through the swirling mist in his head. He could feel his mind submitting to that of the woman, and he knew that she was irresistibly lovely. To his fevered imagination, she was standing before him, naked, inviting yet forbidding in her authority over him. Her breasts filled him with mad desire and drew him to her like magnets, yet he was not able to stir a muscle. He could scent her aroma, and he longed to plunge into the moist softness of the woman. In his drugged state, he was marvelling at her long, slender legs at the same moment as the satin perfection of her delicate arms and shoulders intoxicated him. She was utterly enthralling, and he felt himself to be completely in her power. She ceased her chant and spoke to him, a sultry, exotic goddess who must be obeyed.

'Now, you will do as I tell you, won't you?'

'Yes,' he croaked, unable to keep his vocal cords under control.

'So, now you will give me the Golden Phallus.'

'No.'

'What?' Isis cried. 'How dare you try to hold out against me!'

Donald desperately wanted to explain. With a super-human effort, he managed to blurt out, 'I can't. I don't have it.'

124

There was a pause, during which he was aware that Drummond was urging Isis to hurry. Then she wheeled back to him, and in a honeyed tone, she ordered him to tell her where they could find the phallus.

Alec McFee had left in such a hurry to get to the phantom dog in the Cathcart Road that he had driven some way before he realized that after Donald had returned from visiting his mother, he had not replaced Alec's medical bag in the car. With an oath of annoyance at his brother's thoughtlessness, he swung the car round and headed back to his house. He let himself in and strode into the parlour-consulting-room where he knew that he had left his bag. As he came through the door, he shouted, 'Donald, you are a bleeding nuisance.' Then, as he regarded the chaos in the room, 'God Almighty, what's going on in here?'

Donald was on the point of telling Isis that he had taken the Golden Phallus to Halevy in Paris, when he became aware of the presence of his brother. He saw one of the toughs lunge at Alec, but he tripped over a piece of the wreckage which littered the floor, and the vet struck him as he fell. The place erupted in wild confusion and noise. Alec was hitting out at his assailants, but he was being overwhelmed by the three men. The violence around him cleared the fog in Donald's brain with the shock of a douche of cold water. He took in the scene and hurled himself at the nearest of the toughs. Donald got in one heavy punch, and then fell back in agony as a heavy boot crunched into his knee.

'Quick! Out of here before the racket brings in the neighbours,' ordered Drummond. 'We've got as much as we can out of him.'

The intruders rushed out, but one of the toughs delayed long enough to kick Alec in the stomach as he lay, half-conscious and bleeding, on the floor.

The pain in Donald's knee was excruciating, but he dragged himself over to where Alec was retching and gasping for breath. It was several minutes before they had recovered sufficiently to attend to their injuries. Alec smeared an ointment on Donald's leg.

'It's meant for horses,' he said, 'but it will do until we get you to a hospital. It should ease the pain, but I doubt if you will win the Derby. I must say that I did not care for the manners of your friends. Do me a favour and don't invite them again while you are staying here.'

# 9
## Wolves in Sheep's Clothing

Cleo Janis, sitting in her air-conditioned room in the Ibari Hilton, had been waiting impatiently for her call to Los Angeles to be put through. Although she had left her business in the capable hands of her junior partner, a woman with whom she had worked ever since she had launched herself into the pop world, she liked to make sure that things were under control during her protracted stay in Salamba. She was missing the Californian scene, the bustle and the ballyhoo, the stars and the studios, the sea and the smog. But Isis had ordered her to remain in Ibari and co-ordinate contacts between the raiding parties in Britain and Egypt, as well as keeping an eye on President Milos, and since that fantastic experience in Bali, Cleo Janis knew that Isis had to be obeyed. So, making the excuse that she was suffering from strain, she had told her office back home that she was taking a round the world trip, and each time that she called, she pretended that she was in a different city.

The phone shrilled, and she picked it up hurriedly.

'Miss Janis, your number is ringing,' said the girl on the switchboard.

Cleo told her partner that the weather in New Zealand was perfect and that she was enjoying her rest. There were no problems back in LA, so Cleo promised to call again from Fiji in a couple of days, and hung up. It would be another ten hours before Josef Grunwald was scheduled to phone from Cairo and report on his party's progress in tracking down the newly discovered Golden Head. Two hours later, Isis and Andrew Drummond were due to ring. After taking a leisurely lunch in the hotel, Cleo Janis, as had become her custom, paid a visit to the presidential palace to attend on Milos.

She found the head of the Salamban state in a more mellow and reflective mood than usual. There was a quiet inner strength about the man which appealed to her, and she could tell that she had made an impression on him. Although she had lost the fresh blush of youth, she had matured into an attractive woman, endowed with the sort of good looks which so often go with success.

'So what is the latest news from Isis?' Milos asked.

'I have heard nothing yet today. Isis told me yesterday that they were keeping Donald McFee under observation in Glasgow.'

'Is Sandra Mitchell with him?' Milos could not keep a note of anxiety out of his voice.

'Neither Isis nor Andrew Drummond have even mentioned her,' Cleo assured him. 'I guess that she must have stayed in London.'

Milos was silent, and Cleo knew that she had not succeeded in allaying his disquiet completely. She would have liked to have been able to comfort him, and she suddenly realized that she was wishing that she could go to bed with him, as much for her own enjoyment as for his solace.

'Tell me something about yourself,' she coaxed. 'However did you get involved in Salamban politics? You don't have any African blood, do you?'

Milos laughed. 'No, I am a pure-blooded Yugoslav, if there is such a thing. I was a student at Zagreb, and later at the University of Vienna. We were all revolutionaries in those days, and I joined up with a group of anarchists. But you know, Cleo, they were such silly little romantics. What was their way of bringing in the workers' paradise? Firing a pistol at some so-called fascist politician and usually missing, or planting a bomb which, if it went off, killed the sort of ordinary people they were supposed to be fighting for. Not that I object to terrorism, I used it myself to get into power. Strike where the enemy is weakest, that's what Lenin said, but our wild young kids thought that they knew better. So, while they were getting themselves killed by the police in Europe, or shopped by some undercover cop and stuck into jail for the rest of their days, I calculated that Africa was ripe and ready. With my background and experience, it was not difficult for me to become the leader of the local bands here in Salamba.'

'You know, I don't think that you were ever a real revolutionary at all,' Cleo told him.

'Oh yes I was,' Milos contradicted. 'Living out in the jungle, I was alive, surrounded by true comrades, not the claque of courtiers who infest this palace, all of them on the graft. But I have taken a liking to you and I shall confess something in confidence. Although I have fulfilled my wildest ambitions, and all the wealth and all the women I could desire are mine for the asking, deep down inside me, I am bored. It is as though some part of me has died and shrivelled up. All the thrill has gone out of my life.'

'But now there is Isis, and all that will change,' Cleo objected. 'Once we have the statue of Osiris complete, and installed in the temple here, you will get back your old zest for living.'

'Who are you kidding?' Milos retorted. 'If you really want to know, I don't believe a word of all this nonsense about the Golden Phallus. But if your sect has its centre here, I reckon that it will bring in a flood of tourists with more money than sense, and that's fine with me. However, first of all you have got to get your hands on the head and the phallus.'

'Isis will not fail,' Cleo asserted.

'We'll see.' Milos was unconvinced.

'While Isis is away, can't we amuse ourselves together?' Cleo suggested, and she smiled invitingly at him.

'I think that it ranks as treason to attempt to seduce a head of state,' Milos answered sarcastically. 'I am sure that you have something better to do with your time.'

Cleo flushed. She was not accustomed to being brushed off, and she jumped to her feet.

'I did not mean to annoy you,' she said angrily. 'I'll be getting back to my hotel.'

'No, no, sit down. I'm sorry, that was uncouth of me,' Milos apologized wearily. 'I've not been myself lately, not sleeping properly and everything gets on my nerves. I don't know what is the matter with me.'

He was not telling the truth. Every passing day, the memory of Sandra grew more poignant, and his obsession with her more compelling. The prospect of tumbling Cleo between the sheets would normally have kindled his latent libido, but in his present state of mind, his penis had contracted the dangling disease. He knew that he had to break free, but how? Ever since his outburst at the Isis orgy, he had been forced to recognize that he was not strong enough to cure himself unaided.

'Maybe you could do with a vacation, but you should see a good doctor, and I know just the right guy, a nerve specialist in California,' Cleo told him. 'Can you get away for a consultation with him?'

'It would not be easy.'

Nevertheless, she had planted a thought in his mind. Milos's contact was not an American physician, but a former fellow student in Vienna, who had become an outstanding psychiatrist, and might be able to exorcize the demon in his brain.

Cleo went over to him and stroked his brow, as if

130

she could wipe away his worries. He shook his head impatiently.

'Excuse me for a minute. I want to hear a news report that is about to be broadcast. I need to see how a press release from my office had been handled.'

He walked over to a radio, switched it on and listened intently to the bulletin. He was on the point of turning the set off again when they heard the announcer report the theft of a recently discovered archaeological relic in Egypt.

'This head of the god, Osiris, had some unique features, and the Department of Antiquities is confident that it will be able to recover it soon,' the announcer concluded.

Cleo whooped in delight. 'That will be Josef. I told you: Isis is invincible. Doesn't that cheer you up?'

So exuberant was her joy that she hugged Milos and kissed him fervently. His response was a disappointment to both of them.

That night, Cleo waited in her room for the call from Cairo. It was late, and she was in a fever of anticipation for details of Josef Grunwald's coup. When at last he did get through, she was stunned by his words.

'What? But I heard it on the news bulletin,' she wailed.

'It has been stolen, but not by us,' confessed Grunwald. 'Someone got in before us.'

'My God! Isis will have you castrated,' she breathed vehemently.

'Hold on,' protested the threatened banker. 'We know who took it, some Italian gangster, called Astoli. He runs all the rackets in Rome, and was spotted coming into the country a few days ago with an entire hit team, a huge black muscle man and some fancy doll. He could not possibly have got it out of the country yet, and so it is a race between the police and us to find him.'

'You had better win that race if you want to keep your balls,' Cleo menaced.

About an hour and a half later, Isis herself was on the phone, and was as displeased by Josef's failure as Cleo had forecast, but she had her own bungled attempt to retrieve the Golden Phallus from Donald to report.

'What are you going to do now?' Cleo asked.

'The next step is obvious.' Isis's tone was controlled and implacable. 'The boy does not have it, so it must be with the girl. We are returning to London, and we shall have to find some way to trace her. As she is a pop singer, she must have an agent.'

'You had better let me handle that,' Cleo told her. 'After all, it is my job. I know everybody in the showbiz world.'

'Fly out tomorrow and report to me at the Dorchester Hotel. And do not tell Milos that we are going to deal with his dream girl. We don't want him taking fright.'

It had to be Friday the Thirteenth, and it was a day which Sandra swore that she would remember for the rest of her life. The sequence of calamities started shortly after midnight in the club where she had been engaged to sing. She was still in her dressing-room when the police arrived. There had been a tip-off that the place was being used by a ring of heroin traffickers. Everybody on the premises was subjected to a body search. Sandra, with a batch of other women, was bundled into a van and taken to a dismal, cold police station where they were lined up against a wall, while their handbags and purses were examined. Then, one by one, they were led into a cubicle in which there stood a solitary chair on which they were ordered to place their clothes, after they had stripped to the skin.

Sandra was confronted by a stony-faced matron in her

late forties, who glared at her in official disapproval. While she stood shivering in the draughty cell, the heavy, mannish policewoman carefully examined every stitch of her clothing, bending her shoes to make sure that there was nothing hidden within the soles, running her finger along the seams of her blouse and her underclothes, and virtually dissecting her jeans. Apparently disappointed at her futile search, she beckoned to Sandra to come over to where she was standing. Sandra remained where she was, her arms folded. The tight-lipped harridan frowned: she was accustomed to the docile obedience which was due to the forces of law and order. The two women stared at each other with mutual distaste and hostility. It was the policewoman who gave way. With a grunt of annoyance, she strode over to Sandra, pulled up each arm in turn to look under her armpits, and then ordered her to bend over. As she parted the cheeks of her arse, and peered within, Sandra called over her shoulder, 'Butch bitch, aren't you!'

'One more crack from you, and I'll book you for insulting behaviour, you trollop.'

'Have a good sniff, while you are about it,' Sandra taunted, and she stuck out her buttocks provocatively.

To her amazement, she felt the woman's finger probing into her vagina and lingering there far longer than was strictly necessary. Their bodies were close together, and she could feel the coarse cloth of the uniform against her skin, strangely stimulating, as was the sound of the older woman's heavy breathing. The finger was turning slowly, moving deeper, pressing into her yielding flesh. Sandra squirmed away, and stared accusingly at her. There was a faraway look in the policewoman's eyes, as if she were in a sort of trance. Her features had softened into a sadly wistful expression. She seemed to be remembering what it had been like long ago, before some lover's rejection had soured her. She shook her head violently and pulled herself together.

'Get dressed,' she snapped.

'Do you masturbate all the girls?' Sandra enquired innocently.

'That's enough of your lip! And I would not think about making a formal complaint, if I were you. Nobody here would believe you, and you would make some dangerous enemies.'

The fierce old dragon was quite her normal self again.

The club did not reopen that night, so Sandra had no opportunity to perform and she went straight home to bed. It was ten when her agent phoned to tell her that drugs had been found, the club was closed and Sandra's contract cancelled. It seemed a natural judgement of the gods that, while she was on the phone, the toast had burned and the coffee boiled over. Not much else happened before midday, when the telegram arrived, telling her that Donald was in hospital. As she had no work now, she called her agent and told her that she would be out of touch for a few days and rushed out to the airport to take the first plane to Glasgow. It was a pity that she had not stopped to read a newspaper, or listen to the news on the radio, so that she was unaware of the twenty-four-hour strike until she actually arrived at Heathrow. Consequently, she caught the night sleeper from Euston a day later than Isis and Andrew Drummond had taken it in the opposite direction.

She took a cab to the house in Kelvingrove, where she was greeted by a bruised and battered Alec who told her of the extraordinary raid on the house.

'I am sure that they were after drugs, you know. People think that we vets must have a supply around the house, and they are less well protected than in a doctor's surgery or a hospital. Donald keeps babbling some nonsense about an international gang. I am sure that he is havering: he's been to too many horror movies, I shouldn't wonder.'

'How is he?' Sandra demanded anxiously.

'Oh, you have no need to fash yourself. He took a nasty bash on his knee and he may have damaged a tendon. With him being a footballer, it's a terrible nuisance, but I assure you, as a medical man, that it will clear up with the right treatment, and that is why he is in the Infirmary.'

'It's less serious for your patients since they all have four legs,' Sandra replied, nettled at Alec's making light of Donald's injury.

Alec drove her to Glasgow Infirmary, and he remained in the waiting-room, a gloomy cavern in the Scottish Baronial-Gothic style, while Sandra went up to Donald's room. Alec realized that his heavy-handed attempt to set her mind at rest had misfired, but at least he had the tact to leave the couple alone together.

Donald was overjoyed to see her, and the two of them drove an over-inquisitive young nurse out of the room.

'They insist that I spend a few days in bed to make sure that there is no strain on my knee,' Donald explained. 'The rest of me is as right as rain.'

'I should hope so,' Sandra asserted, as she slid between the sheets.

'They were after the Golden Phallus, Sandy,' Donald told her. 'I think that we ought to warn Halevy.'

'That can wait for a few minutes,' she murmured. 'Now, don't move your bad knee, will you, darling.'

Her warning was facetiously unnecessary, since not only was the whole area around his knee tightly bandaged, but his leg was suspended in the air by an elaborate cord and pulley contraption, rendering any movement of the afflicted joint impossible. Making love to a man in this condition posed a stupendous challenge, but Sandra's ingenuity proved equal to the occasion. After adopting various positions which would have astounded the authors of the Kama Sutra, they finally settled into an asymmetrical variation of sixty-nine.

There was no time for the protracted courtship of foreplay as at any moment some interfering nurse might come blundering in. Donald lay with his shoulders pressed hard against the bed, rather like a wrestler who had been caught in an unorthodox pin, and the only parts of his body which were capable of unrestricted movement were his lips and tongue. Sandra, on the other hand, although fully mobile, had to take care not to hit her bobbing head against the totem pole of Donald's strapped leg. Yet the very zaniness of their love-making added a piquancy, and their kissing and sucking were punctuated by outbursts of giggling. But there was a growing fervour in their embraces. The old magic was still there, and they were soon oblivious to the absurdity of their position.

Sandra was swaying above his erect penis as though she could draw him out of the bed, and he was straining to meet her. For Donald, it was a delicious sensation, a thrilling vibrancy which ran through the whole of his recumbent body, and he relished the glowing warmth of her soft, sweet crotch. The ache in his wounded knee receded; he was no longer aware of anything other than the ever-fresh miracle of the fusion of their bodies. Sandra too was no longer conscious of her surroundings, and in her mounting excitement she was grasping his buttocks to pull him as close to her as possible. She could feel the approach of their orgasm, a triumphant progress of an omnipotent god, irresistible, imperious and magnificent.

They were brought back to the real world around them literally with a crash. With the last violent jerk of her head against its support, the precariously poised hoist collapsed, and Donald emitted a loud howl as his bandaged leg thumped down on to the bed. Sandra fell sprawling on to the floor, and an alarmed nurse came running in to discover the cause of the commotion. She halted, speechless and indignant, at the sight of the wreckage.

'I slipped,' Sandra mumbled apologetically, 'and I'm afraid that I bumped into that thing.'

She nodded her head towards the ruins of the hoist and pulley.

'It looks to me as if you bumped into *that* thing,' the nurse replied acidly, pointing at Donald's still exposed genitals. 'Cover yourself up at once, man, you are a disgrace!' she ordered in a voice which would brook no denial.

The nurse walked stiffly back to the door, but before leaving the room, she called out to Sandra, 'You should be able to control your appetite for one more day. The damage to your laddie's knee is not serious and we intend to discharge him on Monday. Then you can do whatever you like in your own bed, well out of my way. However, the doctor insisted that the joint be rested and that was why we had him nicely trussed up until you came and tried out your circus act. I suppose we shall be busy for ages, clearing up this mess.'

A very chastened Sandra kissed Donald goodbye, barely brushing her lips against his, in deference to the outraged nurse, and slunk out of the room.

'I'll look in tomorrow,' she promised in an embarrassed whisper, as she went.

'Ay, and I shall stay in the room every second that you are here,' warned the nurse.

'Are you what they call a voyeur then?' Donald asked artlessly.

The nurse sniffed haughtily and flounced out, pursuing Sandra right to the main entrance of the Infirmary.

Not surprisingly, Sandra's Sunday visit was a very restrained and sedate occasion, and it was a great relief to both of them when Donald was in fact free to leave the hospital the following morning.

Back in Kelvingrove, he told Alec and Sandra that he would be obliged to take things easy until the swelling of his knee subsided, and this would of course keep him out of the Rangers' team for several weeks.

'But I am out of work as well,' Sandra confessed.

She recounted to them the police raid on the club in London and its aftermath.

'I may as well stay up here in Glasgow with you for a bit,' she concluded.

'You are welcome to stay here for as long as you please,' Alec told her.

Sandra thanked him, and then said that she had better phone her agent and let her know where she could be contacted.

'I am glad you called,' said Agnes Johnson, her agent. 'Something has just turned up which should suit you perfectly. You know that there is going to be a mammoth pop festival at Stonehenge in ten days' time?'

'I read about it in the papers, but the police will never let them have it there, will they?'

'Probably not, but the fuss about it is marvellous publicity. Not that they need it; there will be hundreds of thousands of fans trying to get somewhere near the artists. I suppose that they will eventually settle in the fields around Stonehenge, even if they cannot get to the actual monument. But Betty Jo Wilson was due to fly over and she has had to cancel. I can get the spot for you. Isn't that great news?'

'Betty Jo,' Sandra gasped, 'why she must be the biggest

138

name in the whole country and western scene! But how did you get it for me? It's not my style.'

'I know that,' Agnes said impatiently, 'but there is a revival in the old, smoochy, sentimental stuff. Ella Fitzgerald's records are all being reissued and they are climbing right up the charts. So, this could be your big chance. You had better get your act together.'

'Sure,' Sandra enthused, 'I'll start working straightaway up here and I'll be back in London at the weekend.'

'Make sure you are,' Agnes told her. 'Oh, and another thing before you go. Some people looked in this morning and wanted your address. I told them that you were out of town somewhere. Shall I let them know where they can find you now?'

'No, you deal with them if it's business. I can do with not being disturbed while I work up my act.'

'And what about me?' Donald asked plaintively, as he overheard her last words. 'Can't I disturb you now and then?'

'You are my act,' Sandra replied.

So they promptly got down to some hard work together.


After her meeting with Agnes Johnson, it was the turn of Cleo Janis to own up to the failure of a mission. She found Isis unsympathetic.

'The reason you are here,' the priestess reminded her, 'is that you claim to know your way around the pop world. Find that slut. I don't care how you do it, but I do not want to see you again until you have an address for her.'

Cleo Janis vanished. The gleam in the eye of Isis convinced her that this was not a time to make excuses or offer explanations. She called Agnes Johnson to see if Sandra Mitchell had subsequently contacted her, but she received an evasive response. Nobody in London seemed able or willing to help her. Then, out of the blue, came a revelation.

She remembered that she had promised to call her office in Los Angeles from Fiji, and she decided that London could just as well substitute for the South Pacific as Ibari. This time, there was an item of news.

'We had a slight problem here, but we coped,' reported her efficient partner. 'That stupid bitch, Betty Jo Wilson, has been and got herself messily pregnant. She is sick every morning, and is even more crazy than usual. She has cancelled at short notice that booking we got for her in England.'

'Why didn't she do something about it before it got this far?' Cleo demanded.

'She says she wants to have the baby. You have no idea how our Betty Jo has changed. She has gone all broody and even started knitting.'

'So what has happened about her slot in the Stonehenge Popfest?' Cleo asked.

'A smart-arse London agent got to hear and has slipped one of her singers in. Some kid who sings slushy stuff and plays a saxophone. She's new on the circuit, so you would not have heard of her. Name of Sandra Mitchell.'

It was an elated Cleo Janis who confronted Isis a few minutes later.

'And you propose that we snatch her at Stonehenge?' Isis said thoughtfully. 'I suppose that we could get into this happening, but with the size of the crowd that will be there, we should never be able to get anywhere near her.'

'We would if we were performing,' Cleo replied.

Isis frowned. 'What are you saying?'

'It's simple enough. I can get a group flown in from LA. Everything will be pre-recorded, and the actual performance is a play-back. On the evening, you and I

140

will substitute for a couple of the group. This Mitchell girl has never seen either of us, so she won't suspect anything. We can take her after she has done her turn.'

'But the show is next week. How can you get a new act on the bill now? And what about the members of your group? Are they going to play along with this switch?'

'No problem,' Cleo laughed. 'I know the guys who have organized this popfest. They will slip in an extra group on my say-so. As for the kids in the group, they will do as they are told, if they ever want to get work again.'

A few days later, the organizers of the Stonehenge event announced that in addition to such well-known groups as The Rotten Maggots, Man and Mouse, The Gorillas and The Wigan Washerwomen, Sandra Mitchell would be substituting for Betty Jo Wilson, and there would be an appearance of the fabulous American group, The Phallic Cymbals.


President Milos experienced a twinge of alarm when he heard of Cleo's sudden departure from Salamba. She had taken a plane for London, and the image of Sandra's ivory pale features, crowned by her golden hair, flashed into his mind. The thought that she might be in some sort of danger threw him into a panic which momentarily paralysed his intelligence. And then his brain began to function again. Cleo was a capable woman, but she had never exhibited the ruthlessness of Isis herself, and surely it was Isis, along with the cold, calculating Andrew Drummond, who were the hit team, absolutely dedicated to the recovery of the Golden Phallus. And they were in Glasgow, concentrating their efforts on the unfortunate Donald McFee.

Cleo had left a message that she had to visit London to clear up a misunderstanding which had arisen in her office in California in connection with a proposed tour by a British group. Possibly that was the truth, although the sceptical Milos had his doubts. But, logically, he could not see that her presence in London would constitute a threat to Sandra. And yet there remained that lingering doubt, that vague unease, which reason could not dispel, the fear that haunts an obsessed lover. And that he was so obsessed, he could no longer deny, at least to himself.

In his mid-forties now, he had endured the hardships of the guerrilla war in the African jungle, and emerged mentally and physically as tough as steel. He had destroyed those who had opposed him with admirable efficiency, and by sheer personal charisma had imposed his will on an entire nation – and a nation where he himself was a foreigner. For a man who was so plainly on the pinnacle of success to become moonstruck over a mere chit of a girl had to be an aberration. In the lucid part of his brain, Milos the intellectual, Milos the politician, understood that, but the fevered mind of Milos the tormented lover refused to accept the promptings of his reason. He was sleeping badly and off his food. At meetings with his ministers, he found it difficult to keep his thoughts on the matters in hand. For a man exercising absolute power, this was a dangerous state of affairs. Since it was politically impossible for him to woo and win Sandra, even if she proved to be willing, he would have to find a way of banishing her from his mind. The idea of consulting the Viennese psychiatrist became increasingly appealing, but it is not easy for the head of a volatile African country to disappear for perhaps several weeks without first making elaborate preparations, and if the news were to leak out that the leader was undergoing treatment for mental instability in a cosy European sana-torium, it would be practically inevitable that Salamba would suffer another bloody uprising. So Milos did nothing.

What eventually spurred him into taking action was the sight of Sandra's name in a British newspaper. When Milos read of her forthcoming appearance in a monster pop festival, to be held as close to Stonehenge as the participants could get, it presented him with a new, and disturbing, thought. In all of his sexual fantasies, Milos had never considered Sandra's role as a professional entertainer. It was an aspect of her personality which he had allowed his romantic imagination to gloss over. But seeing it in print brought to his mind once more the flight of Cleo Janis, who was he recalled somebody influential in the pop world, and was also a passionate devotee of the cult of Isis. Could it possibly be that Sandra was after all going to be in some kind of danger, despite all the assurances of Isis herself?

Asombolo was the only Salamban whose loyalty Milos could rely on completely. For that reason, as well as because of his undoubted intelligence and capability, he had become Milos's right hand man. So, it was Asombolo alone that Milos confided that he was planning a journey to Vienna, for a medical consultation.

'I do not need to stress the vital importance of this being kept secret,' Milos said. 'I shall of course travel incognito, and I reckon that if I am away for only a week or two, my absence can be passed off without too many questions being asked. You can see any civil servants or diplomats, while I can be relaxing in the mountains or on a tour, up-country.'

Asombolo nodded assent. 'You will leave an address or a phone number where I can contact you?'

'No, I shall call you. That will be safer. And one last thing, Asombolo. Since I have mentioned my plan to you and to nobody else, should any rumour of my trip get out, it is obvious whose head will roll, isn't it.'

Maybe Milos's trust in Asombolo was not absolutely complete.

The British newspapers were filled with speculations on the anticipated confrontation of the police and pop fans at Stonehenge. The government had made it clear that they would not permit a stampede around one of the most venerable monuments of Europe. The great prehistoric stone circle had always held a romantic appeal: on Midsummer Day, latter-day Druids greet the sun rising over a stone which might once have served as an altar, a slab on which perhaps human sacrifices were offered to the dark gods. The brooding sense of drama of the site had attracted novelists and film-makers who had used it as an appropriate setting for the tragic climaxes of their works. Now it seemed inevitable that Stonehenge would witness fresh violence, a veritable battle.

But, at the eleventh hour, an unexpected solution was presented. The Marquess of Hampton, the somewhat eccentric scion of an ancient family, who had in his youth played a honky-tonk piano in certain establishments in New Orleans, offered to open up the extensive grounds of his country mansion for the festival. The broad meadows of the Marquess's estate swept down to within sight of Stonehenge itself, so while the police would be ranged in ranks around the stone circle, the kids would have taken up residence in the grounds of one of England's stateliest homes.

Ten miles from Stonehenge stands the city of Salisbury, a picturesque place of Georgian houses and rather formal Victorian residences, grouped around the tall, spired Gothic cathedral and its peaceful lawns. It breathes an air of middle-class prosperity, not at all the sort of place to be contaminated by the proximity of a festival, designed for the vulgar masses. Certainly it would have been surprising if the boys and girls in tattered shorts and T-shirts, staggering under their rucksacks, were to seek accommodation in the expensive and elegant Black Boar Hotel. Several rooms had suddenly been reserved by phone from London a few days before the festival. But when a conservative, black limousine drew up in front of the hotel, and Dr Andrew Drummond, resplendent in a charcoal-grey suit of impeccable cut, strode into the foyer, it would have seemed ridiculous to suggest that he had any connection with the Stonehenge Happening. Much the same could be said of Isis and Cleo Janis, also decorously dressed, when they arrived. On the other hand, the members of The Phallic Cymbals were lodged in a humbler hostelry, outside the city.

It was there that Isis and Cleo listened attentively to the group's act, and learned the routine of the play-back. They rehearsed conscientiously throughout the day, until the leader of the group was satisfied that they were good enough to play their parts in the forthcoming pantomime before the public. Then they returned to the Black Boar, where they joined Andrew Drummond for dinner.

For her part, Sandra, too, was busy putting together her contribution to the festival. It meant working up some new numbers, since the intimate songs of hopeless love, which had been her speciality, were great for cabarets, but not at all suitable for being belted out by a battery of loudspeakers over several acres of countryside to an audience of hundreds of thousands. She had no time for shopping, sightseeing or socializing, but spent her waking hours with the members of her backing group, surrounded by tape recorders, playing back each song over and over again until they had it just right. Unlike The Phallic Cymbals, she was putting her act on live. So

145

it was an agreeable surprise when a few hours before she was due to travel to the verdant parklands of the Marquess of Hampton, Donald and Alec McFee turned up at her front door.

'I thought that I would come and give you a bit of moral support,' Donald told her. 'I cannot resume training until my knee is quite better, so there was nothing to keep me in Glasgow.'

'But what about you?' Sandra asked Alec. 'How will the dumb animals of Scotland manage without you?'

'He is the dumbest animal I ken,' Alec answered, jerking his thumb at Donald. 'Somebody has to watch over him to make sure that he does not get himself into still more trouble.'

'Ay, Big Brother is keeping an eye on me,' Donald agreed.

Sandra obtained passes to get them into the grounds, and the three of them set out for rural England.

It was early evening when they reached the ancient county of Wiltshire. The going was slow because of the convoys of cars, mopeds, bikes and vans which clogged the country lanes, and as they neared Hampton House they found themselves in the midst of walkers who swarmed over the landscape like locusts. A police helicopter hovered above them, and frequently motor-bike patrols wormed their way through the crowds. Before they attained the heart of this human chaos, there was a sign reading PERFORMERS ONLY. STRICTLY PRIVATE. It pointed to a track at the end of which was a gate in the boundary wall. Here was stationed an enormous squad of police, and their passes were carefully scrutinized before they were allowed to proceed.

They were on a drive which wound through the gardens of the house and the park beyond. It had been fenced off by the police to keep it clear of the vast audience, and it led to a similarly segregated field which had been set aside for the performers and technicians. From a distance, the space resembled a human ant heap, a wild confusion of tiny figures in constant motion. As they got closer, they were able to distinguish between man-ants who were frantically rigging up the battery of lights, others who were linking up amplifiers and speakers, and a third group who appeared to be trying to carpet the entire enclosure in cables and tangles of wire. A smaller bunch of superior ants bustled about, carrying clipboards and telling everybody else what they ought to be doing.

At the far end of the field was a hedge in the middle of which was set a gate, leading to the main part of the park. Directly beyond the gate, a wide wooden platform had been erected, and this was to be the stage on which the groups would perform in full view of the crowds all around them. At the moment, however, the platform was completely occupied by yet more ant-electricians and audio engineers.

A preoccupied official greeted Sandra and told her about the latest cancellations and changes in schedule.

'You are on directly after The Phallic Cymbals,' he told her.

'The what?' asked Alec, whose Presbyterian education had not prepared him for this culture shock.

'They are from California,' the official said, as if that were sufficient explanation for any deviation from sanity. 'Over there they are big, and we were going to put them on as a finale to this gig, but they have insisted that they appear immediately before Sandy Mitchell. Strange that, but I guess that they have to leave early to get somewhere to be ready for their next engagement.'

In order to watch Sandra, the brothers decided that they would go through the gate with her, but while she mounted the steps to the platform, they would join the audience below. At the end of her act, Sandra would have to go back into the enclosure, to divest herself of the microphone which was going to be clipped to her shirt, pick up her bag and saxophone case, and check out with one of the ant-officials. Then she would join them in the vast open-air auditorium.

The formally attired Isis trio had quit the Black Boar and, in their dignified car, had driven out of Salisbury to the hostel where The Phallic Cymbals were lodged. The two women were then transformed. They cast aside dresses which had been styled for Fifth Avenue, Italian shoes and French lingerie. Wearing the Cymbals' uniform of leopard-skin leotards and fuzzy green wigs, they were unrecognizable, and Andrew Drummond recoiled in horror at the sight. But his horror turned to furious indignation when he was ordered to change into a pair of canary-yellow jeans and a mauve T-shirt bearing the slogan GIVE THE POPE A VASECTOMY.

'I'm not performing. Why should I undergo the humiliation of wearing this rubbish?'

'You will blend in with the crowd,' Isis insisted. 'Get on with it, and don't argue.'

'No, no, no!' he spluttered. 'I absolutely refuse.'

'It is an order.' Isis's voice was icily stern.

'Hold it, sister,' intervened one of the Cymbals. 'Why don't you let him go as he is? Everybody dresses screwy and oddball, and with that goofy outfit he's got on now, he will be just one more geriatric hippy.'

Isis regarded Andrew Drummond's formally cut suit, striped shirt and silk tie.

'Maybe you're right,' she conceded. 'All right, go as you are. But you will have to stay outside in the car. There's no way we could get you into the performers' enclosure dressed like that, so you will miss the act.'

'That will be my pleasure,' he stated stonily.

The genuine Cymbals drove off in their own car, and the Isis group followed. They met no difficulty in gaining admission, although Drummond was irritated at being taken for a chauffeur.

The start of the event was delayed by the customary breakdown of a generator, the short circuit in the lighting equipment, and a couple of loudspeakers being stricken dumb. However, the audience remained stubbornly good-tempered, sitting and sprawling on the lawns, singing and drinking, mostly soft drinks, and smoking, mostly not tobacco. The police turned a tolerant, blind eye and ignored the twitching of their nostrils. As long as the proceedings remained peaceful, they were content to leave well alone. It was already dusk and the spotlights turned the foliage a ghostly silver. They were supplemented by a battery of half a dozen powerful search-lights, which were intended to criss-cross among the crowd, turning the majestic park into a gigantic roofless disco.

As one turn followed another, the excitement mounted, and by the time Sandra was called, the atmosphere was electric. The Phallic Cymbals trooped back off the stage into the enclosure, and Sandra grabbed her saxophone and started for the gate. Donald kissed her and wished her good luck. Then he and Alec fought their way into the huddled mass of bodies below the platform until they found a spot where they could see.

Sandra was ready to start when a harassed official ran out of the enclosure.

'Wait a moment!' he cried. 'We have to switch the platform mikes back on.'

Sandra looked puzzled, and he explained, as he adjusted the mikes, 'The last lot had to do a play-back. One of the girls has a sore throat or something, but they

149

always travel with their whole programme on tape, in case of accidents. You're OK now.'

Her first two songs were numbers which were already well up in the charts, but her last one had been specially written for her, and for this event. As the music started, two of the searchlights pivoted their beams to play upon the giant pillars and slabs of weathered stone of Stonehenge, standing on a slight hillock and dominating the terraced fields below.

> Stone age gal meets stone age boy,
> In neolithic night, they find their joy
> She warms his cave, he hunts her food.
> Life is hard, but life is good.
>
> But came the night, her fire grew cold.
> Love soon died in days of old.
> In her cave, she waits in vain
> She'll never see her man again.

After the final chorus, she played a mournful arabesque on her saxophone, and the tune echoed away to the distant hills before dying into silence. The searchlights gradually dimmed, and the imposing mass of the temple, older than the memory of man, seemed to slowly recede into the distance, and then disappear. There was an uncanny hush, then the applause erupted – shouting, screaming and wolf whistles from some boys who appreciated her sexy looks even more than her voice.

'Isn't she terrific?' Donald enthused.

'Ay, she's great,' his brother agreed. 'I wonder what a lassie like that sees in a daft loon such as you.'

They waited for her by the gate, but she did not appear.

Sandra had hurried off the stage. She noticed that a couple of The Phallic Cymbals were still hanging about in

150

the enclosure, which seemed odd as she had been told that they were in such a great hurry to get away, but she was unconcerned. Having shed her mike and picked up her things, she turned to go back to the gate. As she walked, she brushed past one of the green-wigged girls, and she felt a sharp, stinging sensation. Everything went black. Sandra crumpled and fell to the ground.

One of the officials knelt beside her and tried to revive her.

'Do stand back and give her air,' he called to the crowd who were milling round. 'I wish these kids could lay off the dope,' he complained, more to himself than to anybody else in particular. 'Will somebody run down to the first aid tent and get some help, please.'

'That won't be necessary,' Isis said. She had stripped off her green wig, and she bent over the senseless girl. 'My brother is a doctor. Here he comes.'

Cleo Janis had rushed out of the enclosure, dumping the empty plastic hypodermic which Andrew Drummond had given her in one of the packing cases as she went. It would be discovered in the morning, but by then it would not matter. Now she returned with Drummond, and the crowd gave way before this authoritative figure. He looked exactly what he was, a highly respected medical man.

He bent down and made a cursory examination of the unconscious girl.

'I can't do anything for her here,' he announced peremptorily. 'Carry her to my car, please. It's just at the entrance.'

A couple of men picked up the inert body and took it out of the enclosure. They laid Sandra on the back seat: Cleo and Isis climbed in, and Andrew prepared to drive off.

The official who had first tried to tend Sandra called out to him.

'Don't go back to the main road. Follow the path down, and you will come to a first aid post in a tent.'

Andrew nodded and set off in the direction which the man had indicated, towards the tent and the mystic temple of Stonehenge beyond.

# 10

## *Lamb to the Slaughter*

The first aid tent was situated round a sharp bend in the
drive, a couple of hundred yards from the enclosure,
beside a lodge which guarded a rear entrance to Hampton
House.

'We don't have a lot of time,' Drummond told the two
women. 'It is important to get to work on her the moment
she wakes up, when she will be most confused and
suggestible.'

He stopped at the lodge and explained that he was a
doctor with a patient in his car, who urgently needed
more sophisticated treatment than the facilities of the
first aid post could provide.

'Go straight on once you are through the gateway,'
advised a local policeman. 'The lane leads past
Stonehenge, and a mile further on, turn left at the
crossroads. That will bring you directly into Salisbury
without getting caught up in the traffic on the main road.'

Andrew Drummond gravely acknowledged the information: the policeman saluted, and they drove out of the
grounds of Hampton House.

'Now,' he mused, 'where can we take her where we
can be sure that we shall not be disturbed?'

'It's obvious,' Isis replied. 'What is the only spot for
miles around which is guarded against intruders?'

The three of them gazed up at the sombre bulk of
Stonehenge, no more than a hundred yards away, at the
end of a wide footpath which joined the lane just ahead
of them. They were well out of sight of the gate and the

lodge: Andrew Drummond swung the car off the road and it cautiously nosed its way along the footpath.

It was the cold that brought Sandra back to consciousness. In the black abyss of her mind, there had penetrated a chill, more intense than anything she had ever experienced. There was a numbness invading her limbs, and she sensed that unless she broke through the veil of darkness, that icy cold would spread throughout her body to her very heart. If she were not to die, she must force herself to open her eyes.

She was lying on a flat, rough stone. Above her, there floated an even more massive slab, apparently suspended from the stars which were staring down impassively at her. The chill of the stone was creeping into the marrow of her bones, and she tried to raise herself, but found that she was unable to stir. In the distance, she could hear the dying strains of a song, and a full-throated roar of thousands of voices, cheering and shouting. The moon came out from behind a cloud, and it threw across her face the shadow of two immense stone pillars which towered above her, thrusting upwards, as if to tear the sky apart. Perhaps she was dead, and this was her tomb, or could it be the entrance to Hell itself?

Two faces peered down at her. One of them was extremely beautiful, but both of them regarded her with an expression as hard and as cold as the very rock on which she had been laid. She wondered why their hair was green: were they creatures from some other planet, or maybe they were demons, sent to carry her through these portals to whatever terrors might lie beyond?

The first demon was talking to her, but it was a few seconds before she had collected herself sufficiently to make out her words. Something about a golden phallus drifted into her befuddled brain.

154

'And then we can make love, real love, burning, passionate love,' the demon intoned.

That would be nice, Sandra thought. It would thaw out her frozen body, warm, comforting love. She was speaking herself now, but her voice was strangely remote, and she did not know what she was saying.

The first demon nodded. She was dressed like a leopard, as was her companion, and Sandra knew that they were beasts of prey who could tear her to pieces. She felt helpless, open to them and completely vulnerable, and yet they were talking to her of love, and she desperately wanted to be folded in their arms and to relax in the heat of their bodies. Perhaps she said so, for the first demon, the impossibly lovely and terrible being from another world, had pulled off her leopard skin, and now was revealed in the perfect form of a woman. She was gliding closer, the alabaster sheen of her flesh, luminous in the rays of the moon, framed by the rugged stone all around them.

Something was moving up her bare thighs, and Sandra became aware that she was lying naked on the stone altar, and that the second demon was parting her labia, and tenderly but insistently inserting her fingers. There was nothing that she could do but submit. Perhaps it was what she wanted, perhaps she had even asked for it, but her head was not together, and she did not know.

Now the first demon was so close that Sandra could smell her. Not some artificial scent from a cosmetics factory, but the rich, tangy aroma of her body, and Sandra felt the uncontrollable gush of her own love juices soaking the questing fingers which were now possessing her. There was a hand on her breast, and her nipple was so tight that it wanted to explode. Even the cold was forgotten, as the two demons methodically roused her lust and took her over.

'That is what you want,' the first demon told her.

She had climbed above Sandra who stared longingly up at the sultry mystery of her cunt, fringed by soft, curly hairs, like an exotic sea anemone, luring her to enter into the sweetest trap and to lose herself for ever. If only she could raise herself and taste the ripeness of that fruit!

Outside Sandra's field of vision, Andrew Drummond anxiously glanced at his watch, and whispered to Isis that she must hurry.

'It is better when we do this with the Golden Phallus, isn't it?' Isis murmured in Sandra's ear.

The helpless girl made a gurgling noise, which gradually resolved into words.

'Like at The Double Cross,' she lisped.

'She's delirious and talking nonsense,' Cleo hissed at Isis.

Isis shook her head. She was getting through, and she knew it.

'Who double-crossed? Was it you?'

She hardened her pressure on Sandra's nipple to encourage her to talk.

'Everybody double-crosses there,' she confided.

'Where was that?'

There seemed to be some impediment in her mind, warning her not to tell this luscious demon, but Sandra concentrated and finally got the words out.

'In Paris. I was with Louis.'

'And with the phallus?' The demon was remorseless, and could not be denied.

The friction in her pussy was filling her with an intense desire to please these loving demons.

'Yes, I brought him the phallus,' she simpered.

'And now, you are going to bring it to us, aren't you.'

They were bending eagerly over her, all four hands

156

pressing, kneading, stroking, caressing, coaxing, compelling, plucking the truth out of her.

'No, I can't. It's in Paris.'

'With Louis?' The first demon's eyes were boring through her. 'Why did you give it to him?'

'He understands Egyptian things,' Sandra explained.

'Got it!' Cleo exulted. 'Louis Halevy, the Egyptologist. He was in Salamba, remember?'

'Is that right?'

There was a new hardness in the first demon's voice, and a flicker of fear went through Sandra. But Isis did not need to wait for an answer. The blend of trust and terror in Sandra's eyes told her all she wanted to know.

'Right. That's it. Now let's get out of here,' called Drummond.

'One minute. Will she remember all this?' Isis asked him.

'Of course she will. The stuff is a hallucinogen, but there is no such thing as a drug which wipes out memory.'

'Then it is too risky to leave her alive.' Isis spoke in a matter of fact tone.

The two women abruptly stopped their erotic handling of Sandra, who felt a chilling tremor of awareness of what she had done, as her brain began to clear.

Cleo burst into hysterical laughter. 'We should kill her. After all, this is a temple, and it is right that she should be offered as a sacrifice to Isis whom she has offended.'

'I have a scalpel,' Andrew Drummond said.

He moved round to look down at Sandra who became conscious of his presence for the first time. There was a strained, sadistic light in his cold blue eyes, and she cringed away from him.

'Poor Andrew!' Isis called mockingly. 'Did our little game with the bitch turn you on? Why don't you have your own fun with her before we get rid of her? Just don't be too long about it.'

It was a risk, but how could he resist the temptation? She was as pretty as a freshly plucked flower, and it would be a waste to throw the blossom away before savouring its fragrance. And what Isis had said was true. The sight of the two of them, seducing and manipulating their victim, had aroused in him a wild fury of lust which had to be quenched. In his state, it would be over in a minute. And then, after he had defiled her, he would have the pleasure of destroying her, so that no other human being would ever possess her again. He unzipped his trousers, and stepped out of them.

With a smile of anticipation on his lips, he advanced on the girl who still lay, motionless, on the altar slab.

'What's keeping her, I wonder.'

Donald looked anxiously at the entrance to the performers' enclosure through which Sandra should have emerged.

'Maybe she's stopped to talk to some of the other artists,' Alec suggested.

The next act was already on, and when it drew to a close and Sandra still had not appeared, Donald's irritation turned to alarm. The two brothers pushed their way into the enclosure once more and looked around them. There was no sign of Sandra. Donald caught sight of the official who had spoken to Sandra before her turn, and he went over to him.

'Do you happen to know what has happened to Sandra Mitchell?' he asked.

The man shook his head in annoyance.

'What she does is her own affair, and I am not prepared to make any statement.'

Donald took him by the collar, and shook him fiercely.

'You had better tell me what's going on. I am her boyfriend, remember? And if she is harmed and I think that you have anything to do with it, I shall break every bone in your miserable body.'

'Steady on.' The official was rattled. 'I thought for a moment that you were one of the scandal-mongers from the press, trying to find something bad to say about the festival. Listen, your girlfriend fainted. Luckily there was a doctor on the spot, and he had her taken away.'

'A doctor, here, in the performers' enclosure?' Alec asked incredulously.

'Well, he was just outside. One of the girls in The Phallic Cymbals said that he was her brother, and they went off together. I suppose that they are down at the first aid tent: why don't you go and look for them there?'

A suspicion began to form in Donald's mind, and to spread like a cancer.

'Tell me,' he said. 'This doctor, did you get a good look at him?'

'Yes. A tall man with glasses, in his fifties, I would guess, and dressed as if he were in his consulting room in London.'

'London? But I thought that the group came from Los Angeles?'

'That's right,' the official admitted thoughtfully. 'But the guy looked British, and when he spoke, I would swear that he was not American.'

'Oh, my God,' Donald groaned. 'I am pretty sure that we have met this creep already, don't you think so, Alec?'

'Come to think of it,' their informant added, 'when the girl spoke, she did not sound as if she came from the States either. Once she took off her wig, she was quite an eyeful – dark and exotic.'

'We have to find Sandy,' Donald cried, 'but if these

folk are who we think they are, she won't be down in some friendly first aid post.'

'Who are these people, Donald?' his brother wanted to know.

'They are a bunch of fanatics, dedicated to some primitive religion or other, with a great line in mumbo-jumbo,' he answered bitterly.

'What, like those Druids?' Alec asked, with a nod towards the dim outline of Stonehenge.

Donald stared at him. 'You know, you might just possibly have something there.'

Without a word of explanation, he sprinted across the enclosure to one corner, beside which was stationed one of the battery of searchlights. His knee ached from the effort, but he could not bother about that now. He called out to the man who controlled the light.

'Swing that thing on to the temple again, like you did during Sandra Mitchell's last number, will you?'

The man started to protest that this would disrupt the routine of the singers who were now on stage, but there was an urgency about Donald's entreaty which convinced him.

The powerful beam of white light lit up the ancient ruins in sharp relief, as if it were a stage. And they saw that the stage was not empty. On the flat altar stone in the centre of the scene there lay a supine form, the naked figure of a young girl. Around her were two women, clad in spotted fur, and poised above her, as if he were the officiating priest, stood a man wearing a formal jacket but, as far as they could make out, no trousers.

The effect of this sudden and unexpected theatrical stroke was electrifying. Perhaps a hundred thousand pairs of eyes turned on to the solemn setting of the primaeval temple, and the actors in the strange ritual which was being enacted before them. Then they burst into wild cheering, in the belief that what they witnessed was one more planned event in the Stonehenge Happening.

Others reacted very differently. Donald and Alec hurled themselves across the enclosure and out on to the drive. Alec was ahead, and pounding towards the first aid post and the lodge beyond, when he heard a roaring at his heels. He just had time to throw himself to the side of the road as Donald hurtled by, mounted on a motor-bike which had been standing close to the entrance to the enclosure.

At the lodge, nobody attempted to stop the racing motor-bike. The police who had been on duty there had seen the dramatic tableau and were on their way to investigate.

But the group who were virtually thunderstruck by the sudden illumination were not any of the onlookers, but those who occupied the stage. Andrew Drummond, hovering above Sandra like a vindictive hawk, was completely blinded and staggered backwards. Cleo, utterly unnerved, covered her eyes and reeled away, screaming. Isis was the first of them to come to her senses.

'Quick!' she cried. 'Everybody will have seen us. Into the car, there's not a moment to lose.'

'What about the girl?' cried Drummond, shaking his head, as he tried to regain his vision.

'For God's sake!' shouted the exasperated Isis. 'Can't you understand? Leave her! There's no time to deal with her. They will be on top of us in no time.'

While she was speaking, she was leading the way to the car parked at the end of the footpath close to the ruins, and her two confederates blundered in after her. By now, Andrew Drummond was wide awake to their peril, and the car was moving before they had time to close the doors. In a shower of mud and gravel it turned and

161

started down the footpath. They had to get to the road below, where they could get lost in the traffic before they were intercepted.

They had almost made it when they met a solitary on-coming motor-bike. Like them, it was travelling very fast, but in the split second that he was held in their headlights, Drummond recognized Donald, crouched over the handlebars like an avenging fury. Andrew Drummond swore and tugged the wheel round viciously. The tail of the heavy car slewed across the road.

The footpath was completely blocked and although Donald jerked the handlebars hard, there was no way that he could avoid hitting the limousine. He caught the rear of it a glancing blow. The bike went spinning into the hedge, and Donald was catapulted over the tail of the car into the bushes and trees which bordered the path.

Andrew Drummond restarted his stalled engine. Apart from a heavy dent, the vehicle was undamaged. He careered down the last few yards of the path, turned the car on to the road beneath, and vanished into the night.

It was some time later when the ambulance got to the scene. Alec had supervised the rescue of Sandra, who lay huddled under a blanket on one of the bunks. They had come upon the wrecked motor-bike and, searching around, Alec stumbled on the unconscious body of his brother. They had lifted him into the ambulance, where he now lay in the bunk beside Sandra's.

Although Alec was accustomed to a different category of patient, he examined Donald's buffeted body. Miraculously, it seemed that, apart from his previously damaged knee, there were only superficial injuries. But when Alec looked at that knee, his expression grew grim. He had sufficient knowledge of human anatomy to know that what had been a simple swelling of the joint had been transformed into something far more serious. It would require a specialist to give a proper diagnosis of the footballer's condition, but Alec doubted whether he would ever play again.

# Part III

# 11

## *The Sitting Duck*

'Do you think that the ancient Egyptians ever used this thing?'

Petra held the Golden Phallus in her hand, and turned an enquiring gaze on her tutor and lover.

'Do put it away, dear, where I told you,' Halevy replied. 'Even the sight of it makes me feel nervous.'

'It makes me feel sexy,' Petra pronounced. 'Let's keep it out for a few minutes. You will have to go soon, so an extra stimulus won't do any harm.'

They were sitting in Petra's room in the students' hostel, and Louis Halevy, like all other visitors, would be required to be out of the building at midnight. Although the old-established rule was no longer strictly enforced, it was observed by members of the teaching staff to avoid encouraging the rumours and scandal-mongering which enlivened the academic routine at the Sorbonne.

The Professor kissed his passionate student.

'I have a research project for you,' he told her with a smile. 'I shall persuade the Faculty to publish an issue of *Penthouse* in hieroglyphics, and I shall leave you a free hand with the illustrations.'

'Let me show you what I can do with a free hand,' Petra purred.

'I adore your hands,' Louis Halevy said fervently. 'So slender and so agile. And yet, so strong and capable.'

But while he held one of her hands by the wrist and kissed each finger in turn, her other hand was fully occupied below. Avidly and purposefully, it grasped his balls, and as though she were a snake charmer summoning

167

a cobra from a basket, the spell of her nearness drew his penis erect, like a reflection of the Golden Phallus itself, snugly reclining under Petra's mauve panties which she had pulled off and tossed aside.

Despite the difference in their ages, they were very well suited to each other. Petra had, during her revolutionary days, had enough of impulsive young men, sexists who believed themselves to be heroes, entitled to take any of the women, whose function in their view was simply to serve them. Louis was different. His idea of pleasure was giving her pleasure, and she warmed to him. She admired his enormous intelligence, but even more was she influenced by the kindness and sensitivity of his personality.

They made love on her narrow single bed. The touch of his hands upon her body brought goose-bumps to her skin, and her mouth sought his as if she could drink the very soul of her lover, while he went on stroking her smooth flanks. With Louis, having sex was an act of worship: everything he did made her feel so good. They were lying side by side: she held him tight inside her, warm, pulsating, at once possessing and possessed. The blood in her veins was singing for sheer joy, and as she felt his muscles stiffening and she knew that their climax was near, her hand stretched out. Without realizing what she was doing, she grasped the Golden Phallus. To her fevered senses, the metal seemed to be throbbing, and warm to her touch, and it was as though it joined them in their orgasm, the symbol of gratified desire.

They dressed unhurriedly, and went, hand in hand, out of the hostel to a nearby café, where they took a leisurely coffee. Then Petra went back to her room – she had an essay to prepare – and Louis Halevy returned to his own apartment.

He had been home for half an hour when the phone

rang. It was Sandra, but a very different Sandra from the girl who had been his Juliet at The Double Cross, or strolled through the forest of Fontainebleau. She told him of the attacks on Donald and on herself by Isis, and tearfully owned up to having disclosed his name to the enemy.

'Please forgive me, Louis,' she sobbed. 'I can't explain what happened, but I could not help myself. They must have given me some sort of drug. And then, they were going to kill me, I swear it. I must have put you in great danger.'

Halevy was calm and his voice reassuring. 'When did all this happen?'

'They took me to Stonehenge last night. I called you as soon as I could. It was hours before I was able to move and speak.'

'What about Donald?'

'He is in hospital. It seems certain that he will have to have an operation on his leg. I don't understand the technicalities, but he is going to be examined by a world-famous specialist, another Frenchman, as it happens.'

'Keep me posted,' Halevy said. 'And, Sandra, thank you for the warning. Don't blame yourself: I am sure that there was nothing that you could have done, and don't worry about me. I can look after myself.'

But after she had hung up, his face was grim, and he concentrated on how best he could deal with the threat which was overhanging him – and the phallus.

The British newspapers carried garbled accounts of the events which had enlivened the Stonehenge Popfest, and their readers soon lost interest. Neither Sandra nor Donald, in their respective fields, had yet achieved star status; they were still considered promising youngsters, so their exploits never dominated the headlines. And the

169

police did not follow the trail of Isis very far. The official view was that the scene at the altar stone, so starkly illuminated by searchlight, was nothing more than a staged publicity stunt. Of course, Sandra had been insensible when she had been loaded into the ambulance, but what could you expect from some irresponsible teenager who had been high on drugs? As for Donald, he was the victim of just one more hit and run accident, and there was practically no hope of tracing the car or the driver. The police had far more important problems to deal with than combing the country for members of a conspiracy which, so they suspected, only existed in the over-active imagination of a pop singer, anxious to thrust herself into the limelight.

In Dr Andrew Drummond's discreet Regency house, overlooking Hampstead Heath, the woman who was Isis reviewed progress and made preparations for the next operations. A telephone call to Cairo had produced another piece of information from Josef Grunwald. Moriba's associates had been less than efficient: a corpse which had been washed ashore on a beach near Port Said with its hands and feet bound had been recognized as the mortal remains of Pino Astoli.

'And the Golden Head?' Isis demanded.

'So far, there is no sign of it,' Grunwald admitted. 'It looks as if the theory that it had been stolen by Astoli might be wrong.'

'Of course it is wrong,' Isis hissed. 'The police were fooled by the true thief, and you were an idiot to believe them. It is certain to have been smuggled out of Egypt by now, so you might as well get back to Ibari where we can remain in contact with you, and you can keep an eye on Milos.'

'This guy Halevy,' Cleo said, after Isis had given

170

Grunwald his marching orders. 'We know that he has the Golden Phallus. Maybe he took the head, too?'

Isis shook her head impatiently. 'He is a scholar: this was the work of a professional criminal. But he might have a shrewd suspicion of the identity of the thief, and give us the lead we need. Some of us had better pay the good Professor a visit.'

'But this time, there must be no mistake,' Drummond warned. 'Let us put a watch on this Halevy and get to know all about him before we strike.'

Isis agreed. 'You and I will go to Paris and deal with him at the appropriate time. As for you,' she added, turning to Cleo Janis, 'your usefulness here is finished, and you have no part to play in Paris. You will return immediately to Ibari and resume your former duties.'

Asi Moriba was in good spirits. Ever since his return to Rome, he had been gathering up the reins of power over the various underworld rackets which had dropped from the lifeless hands of Astoli. His ruthlessness had crushed any stirrings of revolt, and the efficiency with which he had despatched his predecessor endowed his reign with a kind of jungle-law legitimacy.

And, of course, there was the Golden Head of Osiris, probably worth a fortune, and safely in his possession. But Anna was dissatisfied. She had quit Ibari, and Milos's bed, in search of the Golden Phallus, and as long as that eluded her, no other prize would compensate. As usual, things came to a head between them in the bedroom.

A pretty little country girl had been picked up by one of Moriba's talent scouts as she came out of the main railway station. She had looked around her with the bewilderment of a simple soul who had never before ventured into the Big City, and had no idea where to go or what to do. This was a place where pretty girls became beautiful stars and fabulously rich, but how to set about this transformation? So she had been grateful to the kind gentleman who had walked up to her, and without any formal introduction had offered to show her to a cheap pension. He had taken her in his own car, and throughout the ten minute drive his conduct had been absolutely correct.

But what had excited her was not what he had done, or had not done, but his words. He explained that he had just happened to be there when she came out of the station, and he was able to spot her predicament because in his job he had grown accustomed to summing people up at a first glance. He was an assistant film director, and was responsible for casting minor roles. Many of the young hopefuls whom he had placed in a small part in a second feature film had gone on to become world-famous celebrities. What they had needed was to set their foot on the first rung of the ladder of success, and that was what he had achieved for them. As they entered the pension, and this glamorous stranger was on the point of disappearing from her life for ever, his gullible victim babbled her thanks, and added that she also wanted to get into movies. He had looked at her with a critical, but appraising, eye and eventually told her that she was a pretty chick, and that it was just possible that he might be able to help her in the next few days.

So it was that, in her only good dress and wild with excitement, she had been delivered to Moriba who, she had been informed, was the real big shot, the man nobody ever heard about who controlled the whole entertainment industry. The luxury of his home dazzled her, and she knew without a shadow of a doubt that by a fairy-tale stroke of fortune she had penetrated to her eldorado. That the magnate turned out to be a black giant came as something of a shock, but when she saw Anna, her confidence was restored. If a woman as lovely and as self-assured as this could be on easy and familiar terms with the boss, everything must be all right.

'Bettina, that is your name?' The man's voice was deep and powerful, but not unfriendly.

'That's right, sir, and I want to act in movies,' she stammered.

The great man nodded majestically. Bettina stood before him, awaiting his verdict, as she might have attended on the village priest to whom she habitually confessed.

'Take off your clothes,' the man ordered.

Bettina blushed scarlet, and gazed about her in horrified confusion.

'How can you expect to get a part if we do not have a chance to see what sort of body you have?' Anna asked.

The way this woman put it, the command to strip sounded reasonable. She had been taught that to bare her body before another was a sin, but now she could see that it was nothing more than a professional requirement. After all, she had taken off her clothes when she had visited the doctor and this was much the same.

But the doctor had never grabbed her naked body and thrown it on the floor. She had wanted to scream, but the lovely lady had clapped her hand over her mouth.

'Don't struggle,' she advised, 'that makes it hurt much more. And don't be foolish. Every film star has to undergo this initiation. And you do want to be a star, don't you.'

The man had peeled off his own clothes and he stood in front of her, superb in his male arrogance. She gasped in awestruck terror, and she ceased struggling. The thought flashed across her mind that this might be the Devil himself, and she hastily made the sign of the cross over her nude body. But he simply laughed at her. Satan

173

would have shrunk away: this being was even more potent than Satan himself. There could be no power in heaven or on earth which could protect her. With a groan of dismay she submitted, and made no attempt to resist as he sternly pushed her legs apart.

'That's better,' the lovely woman told her, and she stroked her forehead, as one might comfort a child. 'You must understand, this is for your own good. We have to destroy your pride, otherwise you will never be able to handle fame and publicity. Now, do as you are told.'

Bettina wanted to believe: she knew that she had no choice but to obey. She shrank away from the towering colossus. The strong smell of his sweat was suffocating her, and then came the sharp, tearing pain as he forced his way inside her.

'Is it the first time?' Anna asked sympathetically.

Bettina sobbed and nodded.

'Here, suck on this,' she said, unbuttoning her blouse and thrusting her breast at the prostrate girl. 'You will find that it will help.'

Bettina could feel the trickle of blood between her legs, but there was nothing that would deter the giant who was raping her. The woman's smooth, beautifully formed breast was comforting, and she took the nipple between her lips gratefully.

But now, their four hands were gripping her tight, holding her down, and Anna was no longer offering her tit, but thrusting it hard into the girl's mouth, while Moriba was penetrating deeper and deeper. She could not stir a muscle. Bettina was no longer a woman, but merely a passive receptacle, obliged to accept whatever her masters imposed on her. She knew that she was there for their lust to ravish; not only was it impossible for her to offer physical resistance, they had so thoroughly vanquished her spirit that even mental opposition to them

174

was futile. When she felt the hot spurt of Moriba's sperm, she made no attempt to move against his overmastering organ, but meekly accepted his domination.

She lay still, her eyes staring blankly into space. After the two of them had risen from her body, Anna threw her a box of tissues.

'Clean yourself up a bit,' she ordered.

Bettina automatically mopped between her legs, but lay passively on the floor, until Anna pulled her to her feet and gave her back her clothes.

'It will be worth it,' Anna confided. 'We are going to ship you out to a place called Salamba, where we have a film crew working. Cheer up, Bettina, you have made it: you are in movies.'

The girl said nothing. Her eyes were dull and there was a weariness in her movements. It was as though in the last ten minutes she had aged by fifty years. Perhaps she had some intuition that what awaited her in Africa was a role, not in a film studio, but in a bordello from which she would never emerge. Without saying a word, she accompanied the 'talent scout', who had already collected her few belongings from the pension, accepted the false identity card he had prepared for her, and let him escort her on to the Alitalia flight for Ibari.

As the door closed behind her, Anna shook her head and protested to Moriba, 'It's no good. It's just not the same.'

'What are you talking about?'

'That head. I was watching it all the time, but it is dead; it does nothing. I tell you, Asi, we must get hold of the phallus.'

'I'm not that worried. This Golden Head must be valuable.'

'Who is talking about money?' Anna flared up. 'Can't

you understand, you savage, the phallus is magic; it is power!'

Moriba strode over and slapped her so hard across the face that she reeled against the wall.

'Keep a civil tongue in your head, you bitch, or you will end up with Bettina.'

Anna relapsed into a sullen silence. Suddenly, Moriba's features relaxed into a smile.

'Very well, let us see if we can track down your fetish of gold, and perhaps some other parts of this artistic jigsaw puzzle.'

'What do you mean?' Anna asked.

He answered with a shrug of impatience. 'Isn't it obvious that if we have found a phallus and a head, somewhere there must be the rest of an entire statue? And that means that there are people who will be ready to do business with us, if we can trace them.'

'You mean that we shall be able to buy the phallus?' Anna demanded disbelievingly.

'Not at all. I mean that there must be someone who will be eager to pay whatever I ask for the Golden Head. Tell me, wasn't there some famous Egyptologist in Salamba, brought in to examine the phallus?'

'Yes,' Anna replied. 'Louis Halevy, but Milos had him searched and every item of his baggage examined before he was allowed to leave the country. He did not have it.'

'I dare say not,' Moriba agreed, 'but it is likely that he knows who did take it, and I think that he would be the right man to approach about the Golden Head.'

'But he will know that you have stolen it. He will have you arrested.'

'Really, Anna! For someone so materialistic, you are incredibly naive at times. I shall arrange our interview in such a way that he will have neither the opportunity nor the inclination to call in the authorities. And you will

176

come with me. Given the right setting, you have considerable powers of persuasion. And just think, it is possible that, by now, he may have the Golden Phallus itself. Now, wouldn't that be exciting?'

Anna's eyes glistened, but Moriba could not decide whether it was due to hope, or plain avarice.

Milos was unmoved by the news of Josef Grunwald's return to Ibari, but when he learned that Cleo Janis was flying in from London, he had her brought directly from the airport to the palace and pressed her for news of Sandra. But all he could glean from her was that Sandra had sung in some festival near Salisbury. The President had discovered during his violent career that being suspicious had kept him alive, and there was an ingenuous quality about Cleo's response which awakened a feeling of mistrust in him. So he had her discreetly shadowed and her phone tapped. That was how he got to know of her conversation with Grunwald, during which she told the Swiss banker of their treatment of Sandra, as well as the disclosure that Louis Halevy had been given the Golden Phallus.

Milos's first reaction was to murder Cleo in as unpleasant a manner as he could devise but, on reflection, he appreciated that the source of the danger was Isis, and it was with her that he would ultimately have to settle accounts. He feared that there might be a repetition of the attack on Sandra, so he issued a secret order to the Salamban Embassy in London that she should be kept under strict observation, and all her movements reported directly to him.

Within a few days, he had news. She had reserved a flight for her and her boyfriend to Paris for the following week. But now that Isis knew that Halevy had the Golden

Phallus, it was certain that she would also be in Paris, and that meant that Sandra was running into danger.

The time had come to take decisive action. Milos summoned Asombolo and told him that he was leaving almost immediately for his consultation in Vienna. It was as Herr Karl Brodsky, a sanitary engineer, that he slipped out of the country. He changed planes three times on the journey, but his ultimate destination was Paris, not Vienna.


'In future, you are not to come to my apartment,' Louis Halevy told Petra. 'We must assume that it is being watched by the gang which hunted down Sandra and Donald and, sooner or later, they will make their move against me. I don't want them going after you also.'

'But Louis, you need protection. Are you arranging to have some sort of bodyguard?'

'Not at all. I believe that these people are the ones who stole the Golden Head of Osiris from Khalid. We have to tempt them out into the open, and the phallus will be the bait.'

'No,' said Petra bitterly, 'it is not the phallus, it is you who are the live bait. Please, Louis, for my sake, drop it. This game is too dangerous.'

'We have been over that,' Halevy answered firmly. 'You must not lose your nerve, darling. You know what I want you to do; please make sure that you do it.'

Petra's expression was one of glum distress.

'Come now, it's not that bad,' Halevy comforted her. 'You cannot come to my place because it would be too conspicuous, but I can visit you from time to time in the hostel where you are only one out of fifty or more students. Now there is something else. Sandra Mitchell called me this morning to let me know that she and Donald will be coming to Paris next Tuesday. He is hobbling about on a pair of crutches, and will be seeing Doctor Serein at the clinic at Neuilly. Serein is probably the best man in the world in his field and if he is prepared to operate, it might save Donald from being an incurable cripple for the rest of his life. I shall of course go to Charles de Gaulle to meet them.'

'Is there any chance of my going with you?' Petra asked diffidently.

'My dearest girl, I am relying on your being with me.'

# 12
## Fox and Hounds

The Rue Achille is a narrow, winding road off the Rue
du Ranelagh, one of the main thoroughfares in Auteuil,
still, despite changes in fashions, the most elegant residential district in Paris. It is no more than five minutes' walk
from the Avenue du Président Kennedy, which carries an
avalanche of traffic at all hours of the day and night along
the bank of the River Seine, but the roar of the traffic is
but a distant whisper under the rich canopy of the plane
trees which border the Rue Achille. Like every other
self-respecting Parisian street, no matter how humble, it
boasts a few small cafés where habitués loiter, sipping
their cups of café crême, munching fresh croissants, and
earnestly perusing their copies of *Le Monde* or *Le Figaro*.

Isis and Andrew Drummond were so occupied, seated
at a table outside the Café l'Univers, on a bright summer
morning. Drummond glanced at his watch and frowned.

'They should have been here by now.'

Isis patted his hand.

'Poor Andrew, you are so tense. They will come:
everything is under control, so relax. Drink your coffee. I
think that you have been suffering from frustration, ever
since you were interrupted at the crucial moment at
Stonehenge. You really fancied that girl, didn't you!'

Drummond scowled. 'Considering that you are the high
priestess of a cult of lust, I think that a few more practical
services would be desirable. We have shuttled half way
around the globe, like disoriented migrating birds, but a
novice in a nunnery enjoys a richer sex life than I do.'

'Don't exaggerate. Remember Bali.'

'Good God, woman, that was months ago!' he exploded. 'And since then, you have not let me come near you.'

'I am a priestess, not a temple prostitute,' Isis replied in a calm, dignified voice. 'When the statue of Osiris is complete, and the goddess, Isis, is triumphant, you will be amply rewarded for your efforts, and for your privations. Just bear in mind what you experienced in the cave at Bali.'

'Mere hypnotic suggestion!' Drummond scoffed.

'I call it magic and so would most ordinary people, but what does the name matter? You scientists use long words, but do you think that you understand what happened in Bali because you give it a high-sounding name?'

'What was written on that papyrus which you read to us?' Drummond asked curiously.

'That is a secret which was passed to me by the last priestess and which I, in turn, shall hand on to my successor. Through thousands of years, it has never been divulged to any man, and I doubt if you would want to undertake a sex change in order to qualify as a candidate for the honour of learning the secret,' Isis told him with a smile.

'Look,' Drummond interrupted, 'they are going in now.'

Over the road from the Café l'Univers, a small van had drawn up, and two men in blue overalls climbed out. They walked into the dignified stone house, which had been converted into an apartment block, and stopped at the small office which housed the concierge.

'Monsieur Halevy?' one of the men enquired.

'Professor Halevy,' the concierge corrected him. 'Fifth floor, but he is out.'

'That's all right. He wants an estimate for having a new burglar-proof lock fitted on his back door. We only want

181

to measure the door and see what sort of lock is already installed. We can do that from the outside.'

'He never mentioned it to me,' the concierge grumbled. 'Take the tradesmen's elevator.'

The two men went up to the fifth floor and returned ten minutes later. The concierge looked up, and they gave him a friendly nod as they left. However, they did not immediately re-enter their van, but walked across to the Café l'Univers. They sat at a table next to that occupied by Isis and Drummond, and ordered a couple of beers. One of the men, sitting back to back with Drummond, said quietly without looking at him, 'The lock is quite straightforward. We meet where we did yesterday at six this evening. You bring the money and we give you duplicate keys to the back door of the apartment. OK?'

'I'll be there,' Drummond said.


Isis and Andrew Drummond were not the only people keeping Halevy's apartment block under observation. Almost next door to the Café l'Univers stood the Café de Londres, and at a table beside the window Anna and Asi Moriba were installed. Anna was moodily cradling a glass of Ricard in her hands, while her companion was drinking a green liquid, a mixture of Perrier and peppermint which, he insisted, enabled him to blend unobtrusively with the Parisian crowds, like any other six foot three black man.

Moriba had open before him a small notebook, in which he painstakingly recorded everybody who went in and out of the building.

'So, tell me, what are we waiting for?' Anna demanded irritably.

'I am in no hurry,' Moriba smiled. 'I have a pretty good idea now of the comings and goings of the residents, and there are precious few casual visitors here. It is precisely what I had hoped, a quiet, secluded block. When I have my little chat with Professor Halevy, I do not want to be disturbed.'

'And just when are you going to have this little chat?'

'Patience, my dear. When I know that he is at home and alone. Meanwhile, we continue to watch the building until I judge it right to move.'

'And then?'

'Why, I go to the front door and ring the bell, like any other civilized person who wants to discuss the disposal of a precious relic with a distinguished scholar.'

'The Golden Phallus?'

'Nonsense, Anna, my sweet. I shall offer him the Golden Head. If you want to bring up the subject of the phallus, you had better make sure that you come with me.'

Anna glared at him, and bit her lip to keep back an outburst of temper.

'You see, Anna,' Moriba continued, 'I have to keep you under observation as well as Halevy, don't I. You are such a loyal person that you would cut my throat or sell me to the cops if you thought that you would profit from it.'

'But you do not have the Golden Head with you,' Anna objected.

'Of course not. To have brought it would have been a foolish error. As it is, only you and I know where it has been hidden. But from the photographs I have, and the detailed description of it I can give, Professor Halevy will have no doubt that I have it. And since he won't know where it is, he will have no alternative but to deal with me on my terms.'

'You know, I don't believe you,' Anna pouted. 'You are bluffing: you are after the phallus as well.'

Moriba chuckled mischievously. 'So, you will have to stick close to me to see if you are right, won't you, Anna? Just think, if you skulk off somewhere to try and play your own game, I might slip in and pull off my deal with the Professor in your absence, and you would be left out in the cold.'

The weekend passed quietly, and on Monday Halevy took his classes as usual. But he had made special arrangements for Tuesday. He took his car from the garage beneath the apartment block and, under the watchful eyes of Isis and Drummond, and also of Moriba and Anna, drove off just like on any other day. But instead of going to the university, he stopped at the hostel and picked up Petra, who was waiting for him in the street. Then, fighting his way through the dense traffic, he headed for Charles de Gaulle.

'You drive on the way back,' Halevy told Petra, as they left the car in the waiting area at the airport. 'Donald can sit in the front beside you: he will need as much room as possible with his bad leg.'

'When does he go into the clinic?' Petra asked.

'This afternoon. We'll go home, have a light lunch in town, and then drive him to Neuilly. Now, when we get back, you will remember what I have told you to do, won't you.'

'Please do take care, darling,' Petra pleaded.

By way of answer, Louis Halevy kissed her.

Half an hour later, they saw Sandra and Donald pushing towards them across the crowded concourse. Although he was using crutches, Donald was hopping with considerable agility, and the two of them seemed to be in good spirits. There was a lot of hugging and kissing, and then they made their way to the car. While they got

184

in, stowing Donald's crutches in the boot, there was yet another interested onlooker.

But, seated in a parked hired car, Herr Karl Brodsky, sanitary engineer extraordinary, was not on the trail of Louis Halevy. Like a knight in shining armour, he was intent on defending Sandra from Isis, and any other dragons which might rear up in her path. True, he did not carry a trusty sword, but he was of the opinion that, should the call to combat sound, the heavy Magnum automatic he had brought would be an effective substitute, even if somewhat lacking in the romance of mediaeval chivalry.

As they drove off, Brodsky-Milos pulled into the traffic and followed them at a discreet distance.

Drummond and Isis had taken up their customary station at the Café l'Univers that morning, and had watched with interest the departure of Louis Halevy. They waited for half an hour, just in case their quarry had only gone to some local shops, and then they got to their feet, crossed the road and entered the apartment block opposite. Isis had prepared a series of questions to divert the concierge's attention while Andrew made for the tradesmen's lift, but this ploy was not needed. The concierge was on the phone, and concentrating on the conversation too intently to pay any attention to the entry of two well-dressed, patently respectable visitors. By the time he looked up, they had disappeared.

Nobody was on the landing, and Drummond inserted the duplicate key into the lock and turned it. The door swung open: the experts who had made the key had assured him that they were fairly certain that it was not wired to an alarm system, and the two of them walked in.

They searched systematically, room by room. Surprisingly, Halevy's desk and filing cabinets had been left unlocked, but they found no sign of the Golden Phallus. After a whole hour, they were forced to admit defeat.

'I guess that there is nothing for it but to wait until the good Professor returns,' Drummond said.

'Everything is ready for his reception,' Isis agreed, drawing a small automatic pistol from her bag.

They withdrew into the bedroom, where they could hear anybody entering the apartment without being seen.

While Isis and Drummond were engaged in ransacking Halevy's flat, Anna and Moriba had been watching the entrance to the block from the Café de Londres. As both Isis and Drummond were unknown to them, they had no reason to suspect that the couple had been on their way to Halevy's apartment. Indeed, having witnessed the departure of Halevy for the airport, they were confident that the flat was empty.

'If he comes back on his own, we go straight in,' Moriba told Anna.

'And if someone is with him?' Anna asked. 'Does that make any difference?'

'I would rather we had our talk without any third party present,' Moriba replied smoothly. 'I have seen him with a girl. If he brings her home, we wait until she goes.'

'Why? We could easily handle the pair of them.'

'You are altogether too impetuous. We play it my way,' Moriba retorted.

Time dragged. They drank cups of coffee, Anna smoked the best part of a pack of cigarettes, and they waited. Anna fidgeted incessantly: she could not sit still, and would have paced up and down the tiny café if Moriba had not restrained her. He sat impassively, and if he felt any inner tension, he gave no sign of it.

'Maybe he has picked up his girl and they have gone away for the day.'

186

Moriba shook his head. 'Unlikely on a Tuesday,' he said. 'And he did not bring anything down with him, no cases or bags. I think that he will be back. If he had met her somewhere, by now he is probably making violent love to her in her own flat. But since the university term has not yet finished, he can't vanish for days on end. So, take it easy.'

Then, suddenly, there was the car, pulling up in front of the block.

Moriba stiffened. 'Now what do you make of that?' he breathed.

Anna peered through the window of the café. She saw Halevy climb out of a back seat, followed by Sandra. Donald emerged with a bit of a struggle from the front, and retrieved his crutches. As the three of them went into the building, the girl who had accompanied Halevy drove off.

'So now we have to wait for perhaps another day to catch him on his own?' Anna complained petulantly.

Moriba shook his head slowly. 'No, this changes things. Those two kids were in Salamba at the same time as Halevy. My guess is that the reason Milos did not find your elusive Golden Phallus when he searched the famous Egyptologist and all his belongings was that he had already slipped it either to that crippled footballer or to his sexy girlfriend. With the three of them together, I think we can be reasonably sure that the phallus is up there. We must pay them a visit.'

'But now there are three of them,' Anna pointed out.

Moriba laughed. 'The boy cannot do much in his condition. You should be able to hold off this Sandra girl long enough for me to dispose of the other two.'

Anna looked at his magnificent physique, and her doubts evaporated.

'Come on, what are we waiting for?' she demanded.

'Sit down a moment.' His manner was one of a man accustomed to command. 'You stated that there were three of them. First, we have to make sure that there are not suddenly four. I am sure that the girl who was driving is the same one I have seen before with Halevy: she may well be his girlfriend and, if so, it is possible that she has merely gone to park the car, and will be back. If we crash in now, we catch the others by surprise, but if she were to come in afterwards, we might be the ones to be caught off balance.'

Five minutes passed without any sign of the girl. Moriba got to his feet.

'Shall we go?' he invited.


'Go in and sit yourselves down,' Louis Halevy said to Sandra and Donald. 'I shall go into the kitchen and put on some coffee.'

In the bedroom, the two would-be burglars listened intently. That Halevy was not alone was obvious, but how many people were with him and how formidable would they be? They heard Halevy bustling about in the kitchen, and then he was back in the living-room.

'Right,' he said, 'coffee will be ready in five minutes.' His tone sharpened abruptly. 'Hello, what's this? Somebody has been in here, I left a sheaf of lecture notes on that table, and they have been moved. And so have the books which were on my desk.'

The door from the bedroom burst open, and Drummond and Isis rushed into the room. Sandra and Donald were sitting back comfortably in deep armchairs, while Halevy was bending over the desk. Donald made a grab for one of his crutches, but Drummond was too quick for him, and pushed him back into his seat. Isis stood with her back to the window, from where she could keep all the occupants of the room covered with her pistol.

Drummond picked up Donald's crutches and moved them out of reach.

'They could be quite useful weapons,' he remarked, 'so it would be better if we removed the temptation for you to do something stupid.'

'I presume that these are the bastards who attacked both of you in Stonehenge?' Halevy said to Sandra.

She nodded.

'And they were the ones in Alec's place in Glasgow.' Donald could barely restrain his pent-up fury, as he gazed into the muzzle of Isis's gun.

'I do not think that any more formal introduction is called for.' Drummond's facetiousness deceived nobody as to his determination. 'We have no desire to harm any of you, so let us collect what we have come here for, and then we can be on our way, and you will be able to settle down to your interrupted coffee before it even gets cold.'

'You don't seem to have minded using violence up to now,' Donald observed scornfully. 'Have you suddenly seen the light and joined the Salvation Army?'

'Shut up!' Isis ordered. 'You were hurt because you got in the way, and if any of you obstructs us now, we shall have no compunction in killing you.'

'So now that my colleague has made the situation crystal clear,' Drummond resumed in a tone of mild reasonableness, 'perhaps Professor Halevy will oblige us by extricating the Golden Phallus from where he has so skilfully hidden it?'

'Whatever makes you think that I am in possession of the object?' Halevy demanded.

Whereas Sandra and Donald were sitting ashen-faced and dour, as tense as coiled springs, their host lolled casually against the kitchen door and viewed the intruders with a quizzical expression, as if he found their threats faintly amusing.

'Stop fooling!' Drummond snapped. 'We know you have it. Your little friend told us so' – he nodded at Sandra – 'and when she did so, she was in no condition to lie.'

'That may well have been true,' Halevy admitted. 'But it does not follow that I have retained so valuable a relic.'

'Nonsense! Only yesterday, you sent a telegram to a Professor Khalid in Cairo, telling him that if he were to come to Paris you would hand over the Golden Phallus to him for the National Museum and confirming that you had it.'

'You are well informed. I do congratulate you.' Halevy remained unruffled and suave. 'And since we are discussing the subject, what about the head of the golden statue of Osiris which disappeared so mysteriously in Egypt?'

Isis started. 'Do you have it?'

Halevy laughed softly. 'No, I do not. But I wanted to find out whether you had it, and it is obvious from your eager reaction that somebody else has stolen it.'

'That's enough, Professor.' Drummond's cordiality began to crack under the strain. 'There is no point in your playing for time; we have watched this block for days and we know that you are not in the habit of receiving visitors at this hour.'

Halevy shrugged his shoulders nonchalantly. At that moment, there was a ring at the front door.

Sandra and Donald looked up hopefully, and for a moment Isis and Drummond hesitated, rigid and watchful. But Andrew Drummond recovered his poise instantly.

'You keep them covered,' he told Isis. 'I shall deal with whoever it is. It's probably some tradesman. And you' – pointing at Halevy – 'will behave yourself and keep quiet, that is if you want your friends from Britain to survive.'

190

He walked to the front door, and cautiously opened it. Standing before him was a statuesque black man and, behind him, a woman as exotically beautiful as Isis herself.

Milos had been fortunate. The parked cars on most mornings formed unbroken lines along the whole length of both sides of the Rue Achille. But he had hardly driven into the street when the car which he had been tracking pulled away, leaving him a space in front of the block which Sandra and Donald had entered. He recognized their companion as the academic who had been in Ibari, and he judged that the man posed no threat, so he resigned himself to maintaining a vigil over the building until the woman who haunted him emerged.

But he had been sitting there for only a few minutes when two other people went in through the front door. He was petrified. He had been looking out for Isis, or some of her agents. He had not anticipated the arrival of the former police chief and dictator of Salamba, together with the woman who had been the mistress of both Moriba and himself. He recalled Anna's obsession with the quest for the Golden Phallus and he knew that the French Professor and his guests would be in mortal danger. He had sufficient experience of both of them to know that Anna was totally ruthless and that Moriba would not have the least qualm about murdering in cold blood to obtain something as important to them as the Golden Phallus.

He leaped out of the car and ran to the door. He stopped short. There were probably at least a dozen flats in the building. He cudgelled his brains. What was the name of that Frenchman? No names were written beside the buttons of the bells for each apartment, but he hurried inside. In the lobby, there stood a range of post boxes, and he frenziedly read off the names. When his eyes fell on that of Halevy, the recollection flooded into his mind. The concierge was in his compartment, and Milos rushed over to him.

'Which is the apartment of Monsieur Halevy?' he called.

The concierge waved to him to wait. Only then did Milos see that he was on the phone.

'Quickly, please, it is urgent,' he pressed.

The concierge turned away in order not to be disturbed. After all, he was not there to help people, was he? Milos waited in impotent fury for what must have been several years, or so it seemed. At last, the concierge replaced the receiver, and with elephantine deliberateness, turned towards him.

'What did you want?'

'What number is the flat of Monsieur Halevy?'

'It is not Monsieur Halevy. It is Professor Halevy.' The concierge was feeling pedantic, and this was the second visitor to slight his distinguished tenant. Such discourtesy was unforgivable.

'Very well, Professor Halevy,' Milos cried. 'What number, please?'

'His apartment is the only one on the fifth floor,' the concierge informed him, now that honour had been satisfied.

Milos did not wait for the elevator, which of course was still at the fifth floor, but started to run up the stairs as fast as his legs would carry him.

Moriba was a man whose reactions were as fast as lightning. He had expected the door of the flat to be opened to him by the man he had been shadowing. Instead there was this stranger, but behind him Moriba glimpsed, not only Halevy and his guests, but a woman

192

holding a gun. Before they knew what had happened, he had lunged into the room, smashing the door against Andrew Drummond, who was knocked to the floor by the violence of the impact and covering the few yards to where the woman was standing in front of the window. Her pistol had been trained on Donald, and she had no chance to turn it onto the terrifying wild man who charged at her. He had grasped the gun and wrenched it from her hand without her being able to squeeze the trigger. A huge black hand seized her and tossed her, as if she were weightless, into the middle of the room. She was too shaken by Moriba's sheer brute strength to pick herself up, but lay stunned on the floor beside the armchair of Sandra Mitchell.

'That's better.' Moriba grinned balefully as he turned the gun back on the amazed Donald. 'Keep an eye on them,' he added to Anna, who had followed him into the room.

'If I knew that I was going to be host to so many people, I would have bought a larger flat,' Halevy commented. 'And you, I presume, must be the team who snatched the Golden Head of Osiris from my unhappy colleague, Professor Khalid.'

'That's right,' Anna gloated. 'And now, you are going to give us the Golden Phallus as well.'

'I don't think so,' Halevy said.

'Oh, I do.' Moriba appeared to find humour in the situation. 'I am going to work on the assumption that either you, my good Professor, or one of your two guests – the ones you invited, of course, rather than the comedians whose performance I interrupted – are in a position to deliver the phallus. Now, I give you a fair choice. Hand over the phallus, or I shoot this charming young lady.'

The pistol was aimed directly at Sandra, who stared

193

defiantly at him, but her face had gone deathly white. From her previous encounter with Asi Moriba, she knew that he would be as prepared to murder her as to squash a fly which was annoying him. Donald started, as if to spring from his chair onto the gunman, but Moriba imperiously checked him.

'One moment, man,' he commanded. 'If you, or your learned friend, try to tackle me, the girl gets it. Understood? Now, if you want her to live, you have five seconds to hand over the phallus, or to indicate where it is.'

Donald turned an agonized gaze at Louis Halevy: Moriba kept his eyes steadfastly on Sandra. His finger was tightening on the trigger.

'Stop!' shouted Halevy. 'I shall get the phallus for you.'

But his words were drowned by the ear-splitting report of a gun being fired in the confined space of the room. Sandra screamed: before their eyes, Moriba's head burst open like a ripe melon, and the fountain of his blood splattered over her and Donald. For an unbelievable moment, the dead giant stood upright; then his knees buckled, he collapsed to the floor, and the gun clattered from his nerveless hand.

When Moriba and Anna had burst into the room, they had not bothered to observe the nicety of closing the door behind them. In the open doorway stood Milos, the Magnum smoking in his hand.

The shock of this latest intervention left them transfixed, as if they had all been turned to stone. Then, with a shriek of anguish, Anna dived for the pistol which Moriba had let fall, but Milos, who had bounded into the room, hit her hard with his own gun, and she staggered away, colliding with a table.

'Get over there, you two!' Milos gestured with the pistol, and Isis and Drummond obediently moved over to

194

the wall dividing the living-room from the kitchen. 'And you!' he ordered Anna, and she slunk across to join them.

'Milos,' she whined, 'I have only been doing what we agreed, before I left Ibari. They have the phallus: you and I can take it together.'

She took a step towards him, but he motioned her back to the wall.

For the first time, Louis Halevy appeared to be ruffled. He had recognized the crazed Milos.

'You must want this phallus desperately!' he exclaimed. 'Why did you not send some of your commandos or men from the Salamban secret police? God, what a risk you have taken! The President of a country breaking into a Paris apartment and getting mixed up in a shooting brawl! You must be mad.'

'What makes you think that I want the bloody thing?' Milos's voice was hoarse, and sweat was pouring down his cheeks. 'Hasn't it caused enough misery? I tell you there is a curse on it: as far as I am concerned, you can exterminate each other squabbling for it.' He turned to Sandra. 'I have come for you,' he said simply.

She shook her head.

'Come with me, woman!' he shouted. 'You're driving me out of my mind. I've had you followed and I flew from Ibari secretly to be with you. Now, I have killed for you. So come on!'

While he was speaking, his eyes were fixed on her, begging her to have pity on him, but at the same time commanding and menacing.

It was Donald who broke the tension. Taking advantage of the concentration with which Milos was regarding Sandra, he had inched his hand out until he had reached one of his crutches. With a despairing effort, he threw himself out of the chair, and with a great sweeping blow with the crutch, knocked the pistol out of Milos's hand.

At the same moment, the room was filled with policemen. They saw Milos leaping back to recover his gun, and one of them fired a warning shot which almost grazed his hand.

'Leave it where it is!' commanded one of the police.

Milos hesitated and then froze, his hand poised above his pistol, covered by half a dozen armed policemen. They went over to the disarmed man, and as they did so, there was the noise of a slamming door. Taking advantage of the distraction, Isis and Drummond had slipped through the door leading into the kitchen. Drummond had seized Anna by the wrist, and before she could protest, had dragged her with them. Once in the kitchen, they had raced out of the back door of the apartment and taken the tradesmen's lift. It was the clang of the lift door which the occupants of the living-room had heard.

Three of the policemen ran out of the front of the flat and took the elevator down to the ground floor. But they had waited until Milos was safely handcuffed, and that brief delay was fateful.

They raced into the Rue Achille, but it was deserted.

'I think that they went that way,' called the concierge, pointing in the direction of the Rue du Ranelagh.

This would have been the logical route for the fugitives to take, leading as it did to the safety of the traffic on the Avenue du Président Kennedy streaming out of Paris. The cops piled into their waiting car, and roared off with lights flashing and their siren screaming. But the concierge was mistaken.

'Let's get moving before they bring in reinforcements,' Drummond said. The three of them swiftly walked out of the Café de Londres, and went along the Rue Achille in the opposite direction to that taken by the police car.

196

Three minutes later, they had attained the station at Jasmin, and the anonymity of the metro.

It was nearly an hour later when the apoplectic patron of the Café de Londres was released from his cellar, into which his unwelcome customers had pushed him.

Meanwhile, upstairs in Halevy's apartment, a touching reunion was taking place. The police had refused to allow Petra to enter the flat until they could be sure that there was no longer any danger. Now, she was in Halevy's arms, sobbing with relief.

'You were magnificent,' he said soothingly. 'They got here just in time: I do not think that I could have kept up the bluff much longer.'

'Bluff?' Donald queried. 'Do you mean to say that the Golden Phallus was not here after all?'

'Of course not,' Halevy smiled. 'Even before the Isis people got the truth out of Sandra, it was obvious that sooner or later they would come after me.'

'So you put it in a bank,' Sandra said.

'Not at all. These bandits were desperate, cunning, and able to bend men's minds and wills. They would have traced it to a bank or a safe deposit and then subverted some member of the staff who could give them access. The only hope was to hide it in some place where it would be totally unguarded, and where they would not think of looking. From that evening at The Double Cross, the phallus has never been inside this apartment.'

'It is nice and snug inside a locker in my hostel,' Petra told them with a grin. 'It is where I keep my dirty clothes for the laundry. We were pretty sure that I had not been spotted with Louis after you had been here to give him the phallus and, even if I had, it would have been difficult to rob the hostel because there are so many people about all the time.'

197

'And the timely arrival of the police. Did you manage that too?' Donald asked.

'Of course. Louis let himself be set up. For example, the way he sent that telegram to Khalid, he did it so openly that anybody who was keeping him under observation must have known about it. He thought that Isis had the Golden Head and that was wrong, but it did not matter. We arranged that if he did not call me five minutes exactly after he had got into the flat, I should call the anti-terrorist police, since they are the quickest. And that was that.'

# 13
## *Stampede!*

It is virtually impossible to hold a conference on most subway trains: the Paris metro is an exception because the trains have rubber tyres on their wheels. Since the fugitives boarded a train in the slack period between the morning and the lunchtime rush hours, they had quite a large part of a car to themselves and were able to talk in relative comfort.

Ever since the grisly moment of Moriba's death, Anna had been in a daze, and she had joined Isis and Drummond in their flight without any protest, although a few minutes previously they had been deadly rivals. All that had mattered was getting away from the Rue Achille before she was captured, and the three of them had been in the same boat. Now, as the train rocked along, decisions had to be taken, but when Isis broke the silence, she did not broach the immediate crisis.

'Did you love him very much?' she asked Anna.

Anna looked at her blankly.

'The black man,' Isis enlarged. 'You were lovers, weren't you?'

Anna sighed wearily. 'Moriba was my lover, Milos was my lover, so were many other men. They have all gone. What's the difference between one man and the next? If Moriba had lived, he would have betrayed me as soon as it suited him – unless I had betrayed him first.'

Isis stared at her in undisguised hostility, but Andrew Drummond broke in.

'In that case, you are not too upset for us to get down to business. In a very short time, the police will have a general alert out for us, and by then we must be some-where safe. You will come with us.'

'Why should I?'

'For the excellent reason that we need each other. You have the Golden Head of Osiris. I have the means of getting us out of here. And we all still want to get our hands on the Golden Phallus. If we work together, we may yet find an opportunity.'

Isis began to object, but Drummond silenced her.

'You too need me to keep you out of some stinking French jail, so you will go along with what I say.'

Isis swallowed her rage. For the first time, she was no longer in command. Her spell had been broken.

'What do you suggest that we do?' Anna asked.

'We get out at the next station and find a phone. I shall call a certain Dr Gaveau. With his help, we can get out of the country.'

'What makes you so sure that this Dr Gaveau will be willing to do this for us?' Isis queried.

'I know a few things about his past which Jean Gaveau would not like to be publicized.'

'Blackmail?' Anna looked at him with a cynical smile.

'Why not?' Drummond replied. 'Your black male is dead. Long live my blackmail!'

Neither of the women laughed, but they did not raise any objection to his plan. They left the train at Trocadéro, and Drummond found a phone in the station.

He was not gone for more than two or three minutes. When he returned, his face was grim and determined.

'Come along. This is the trickiest part.'

He led the way out of the station. As they climbed the stairs to the Place, they heard the howl of police car sirens. Isis shrank back, but Drummond roughly pushed her forward.

'They are on their way to the scene of the crime: they

would not be rushing like that if they were looking for us.'

Their luck held. Among the many roads which converge on the semi-circular Place du Trocadéro is the Avenue d'Eylau, and there is a taxi station where it joins the Place. A cab was standing, twenty yards from the exit of the metro. They bundled into the taxi and Drummond ordered the driver to take them to the Avenue de l'Empereur in Neuilly.

'What number?' asked the driver. He had to shout above the rock music which was blaring out from his radio.

'I don't remember the number, but we want the Villa Rose. Do you know it?'

The taxi driver guffawed. 'I'll say I do! You're making an early start, aren't you?'

'It is a special treat which we are arranging for a very important person. You wouldn't expect me to name names, but if I tell you that where he comes from, oil gushes out of the desert and he is a king, you might be able to make a pretty shrewd guess.'

The driver was visibly impressed. 'I thought that they looked a better class than the regulars,' he said, with an appreciative nod at the two women.

'Where are you taking us, and what is he talking about?' Isis demanded.

'The Villa Rose is one of those hotels where the rooms are hired by the hour,' Drummond explained.

'What?' Isis effervesced in indignation. 'Do I look like a whore?'

Drummond studied her refined features intently. 'With just a little fixing, you could pass.'

The music on the radio was interrupted by a news flash. There had been a terrorist incident in Auteuil. One man was killed and the police were looking out for

201

another man and two women who had escaped. There followed a description which they had no difficulty in recognizing. A special watch was being kept on airports and coastal towns.

'Bloody terrorists!' the driver commented. 'If I had them, I'd tear their guts out, slowly.'

'Well, I don't suppose that we shall meet them where we are going,' Drummond replied jovially.

The driver sniggered and Drummond laughed a hearty, man of the world sort of laugh. The two women regarded them frigidly.

The traffic was beginning to build up, and Anna flinched every time a police car siren approached. However, no attempt was made to stop the taxi, and eventually they drew up outside a modest, three-storey building which displayed the most discreet name-plate, such as one would expect to find outside the office of an old-established law firm or a private bank.

'Villa Rose,' announced the driver. 'And I hope that you have a very enjoyable day, all of you.'

His smile broadened when he saw the tip which Andrew Drummond gave him, but infuriatingly, he waited until Drummond had rung the bell of the hotel and they had entered before driving off.

In the lobby, Anna halted.

What's your game?' she demanded. 'I thought that we were going to meet your doctor friend, and I presumed in a hospital.'

'So we are,' Drummond assented. 'But use your intelligence. There will be a full-scale search for us in progress by now. The cops will question every taxi driver within miles of the Rue Achille. The last place they would expect us to go is a brothel, and even if they do pick up the scent, we shall by then be out of here, and nobody will have been given the address of our true destination.'

'And meanwhile?' Isis asked.

'What does one usually do in a brothel?' Drummond answered with a smile.

The apartment of Louis Halevy was overflowing with uniformed police, detectives in identical non-uniforms, and hard-faced men from the Deuxième Bureau. Statements were made and compared and the remains of Asi Moriba examined as though some fantastic piece of information could be extracted from the corpse.

Eventually Halevy announced that Donald was due in the clinic.

'Impossible!' declared a police inspector. 'He is a material witness to a major crime and cannot leave until he has been examined by a judge.'

'He has to be prepared for an operation in the morning,' argued Halevy. 'If you are worried in case he disappears, I suggest that he is driven to the clinic in a police car, and one of your men can maintain a guard on his room until the judge has had a chance to take his statement.'

So, after Halevy had reminded them that Donald was one of the victims of the attack, and not a suspect, he was escorted by a veritable posse to the Clinique St-André at Neuilly. Neither Halevy nor Sandra was allowed to go with him, since the judge who was to examine them was still doing justice to his lunch, but they both promised that they would visit him as soon as they were free.

The senior inspector was a worried man. Herr Karl Brodsky had undoubtedly killed a man, and should therefore be brought to justice. But now it turned out that the assassin was the President of a state with which France enjoyed friendly relations. Telephones began to ring in the Ministry of Foreign Affairs on the Quai d'Orsay, and even the President was called away from his table at the Elysée Palace.

'Perhaps you can provide us with a rational explanation of the conduct of President Milos?'

The question was put to Sandra, not by one of the legion of police, but by a quiet-spoken diplomat who must have occupied a very exalted post indeed, since even the Deuxième Bureau men deferred to him. They had brought her to what appeared to be an ordinary private house, but she knew that its function was anything other than ordinary. Somewhere in the building, Milos was being detained: he had been hurriedly removed from the police station to which he had been taken as soon as his identity was discovered.

She recalled the look in Milos's eyes as they had led him away. There had been a mute appeal to her in his gaze which she alone could interpret. Wordlessly, he cried out to her for love, for compassion, for release, and her mind went back to their first meeting when she had been the helpless victim of a hijack which he had commanded. There was a magnetism about him which had captivated her, and she had helped him to escape from Moriba's police. But then he had changed when he became the dictator who had supplanted Moriba. Now, when he was once more just a man like any other, she felt again a tremor of that emotion, and this time it was combined with an enormous sense of pity. For it was to save her that he had left Salamba, endangered his position and his very life, and finally killed. But how could she explain that to the keen-eyed stranger who was interrogating her with such tact and courtesy?

'Please, can I go to him?' she pleaded.

The diplomat regarded her thoughtfully.

'Do you think that it might help?' he asked.

She said nothing, but he read her reply in her eyes.

'Alone?'

She nodded.

'I shall arrange it,' he told her. 'But wouldn't you like first to speak with your friend who is in the clinic waiting for you?'

The switchboard in the 'ordinary' house was as large as that of an exchange and within a minute she was connected to Donald.

'Darling, I am still being held up here, and it looks as if I won't be able to get away in time to see you this evening. Please forgive me,' she said tearfully.

'Sandy, that's all right. I am very comfortable, and they are taking good care of me,' Donald replied. 'I shall see you tomorrow, hopefully after the operation. They are taking me down early in the morning.'

She wished him luck, and hung up. Then she got to her feet and followed the diplomat out of the room.

When Donald said that the staff of the clinic were taking good care of him, he was guilty of an understatement. His knowledge of French was rudimentary, and he feared that this might present him with a problem, but to his delight, he found himself entrusted to the care of an Irish nurse. Clinique St-André was small and expensive, but since Dr Serein was one of the consultants, it was here that the doctors in England had recommended he should come for treatment.

He was shown to a room and told to get undressed. Dr Serein himself examined his knee and confirmed that he would operate on it in the morning. Donald settled down with a book, and resigned himself to the boredom of waiting. Nothing ever happens in a hospital, he reflected: it is simply a matter of watching the hours drag past while you wait. Then Maureen came into the room.

Donald found her a welcome sight with her chestnut hair and laughing brown eyes.

'I'm your nurse,' she announced, and her voice had that lilting brogue which could melt a heart of stone. 'We have to get you ready for tomorrow.'

As she took his temperature and blood pressure, she chatted to him. Her fingers were cool and felt good against his skin.

'Did you hear the terrible goings-on this morning at Auteuil?' Maureen cooed. 'And that's not more than a mile or so from where we are standing now. Some strange man got himself shot, and they are talking about the fellow who killed him going around with a gun, as if he would bring death and destruction on everybody, until he was disarmed by a young, crippled lad who hit him over the head with his crutch, and knocked the villain senseless.'

'It was his hand, not his head,' Donald corrected her.

The sprightly nurse looked at him, and a light shone in her eyes.

'Are you after telling me that it was yourself?'

Donald was a modest boy, but he found that he rather liked the thought of being admired as a hero by this girl. He positively smirked at her.

'My, and what a fine, brave one you must be,' she said in a wondering voice. 'And haven't I the good fortune to be caring for you!'

As if to emphasize how deeply she was affected by her stroke of luck, she tenderly stroked his hair. Donald clutched her shapely forearm and gently pulled her towards him. She did not offer any resistance as their lips met, and when he kissed her long and deep, she responded with enthusiasm. Then she pulled away, and gave him an artful smile.

'Well now, we must look after you properly, mustn't

we! I am away to clear up a few things, but I shall be back in ten minutes to shave you.'

Donald felt his chin in astonishment, but the nurse laughed at him.

'Shave your leg, you silly, for your operation. Mind you are ready for me. And I promise you that we shall not be disturbed.'

So, once more, he settled down to waiting, and after ten minutes he was staring eagerly at the door, willing it to open. Another five minutes limped away, and his impatience gave way to doubt and dismay. Had she been playing games, or perhaps some dragon of a matron had intercepted her and sent her away on some other errand. The thought struck him that he was being disloyal to Sandra, even to think of how much he would relish holding Maureen's lissom body against his and how good that first kiss had tasted. He convinced himself that what he was experiencing was a perfectly normal reaction to the violence of the battle of the Rue Achille, which had sent the adrenalin flowing so that he now needed physical relief. It was as though a great pressure had built up within him; his body was stressed for fighting; sex would provide a necessary safety valve. At least, it would have if Maureen had returned.

He had tossed his book aside and was lying back, excited but frustrated and disappointed, when, just as he had given up hope, she was back, carrying a basin and a razor, a towel over her arm.

'You have been ages,' Donald complained. 'What have you been doing?'

'My goodness, and aren't you the anxious one!' she mocked. 'Do you not understand that there are other poor folk in the clinic, lying in their beds and groaning aloud for a nurse to come and minister to their suffering?'

She had closed the door and busied herself arranging screens around his bed.

'Just in case anybody comes in where he is not welcome,' she said. 'I must not lock the door, but screens would give us a few seconds to make sure that we are not discovered in a position which would set idle tongues wagging.'

Donald tried to grab her, but she slipped away from him.

'Now, you must bide your time,' she teased. 'I have come here to shave you, and shaved you will be. Afterwards, if you have behaved yourself, you might be rewarded with a special consolation prize.'

'Just a kiss to keep me going,' he cajoled.

'No, no! What I am worried about is not to keep you going, but to stop you from coming. Now, lie still.'

She pulled aside the bedclothes. Donald was wearing one of those long, shapeless operating gowns, and she rolled it up, baring the whole of his body as far as his navel.

'I thought that you were going to shave around my knee.'

'We always prepare the whole area,' she told him in a serious tone. 'It may be that the poor, darling doctor is not himself after a heavy night and we want to be sure that, if his hand is just a trifle unsteady, anywhere he might chance to cut while he is not fully himself will be wholesome and sterile, don't we? And there is always the chance that if he is pleased with the way he deals with your knee and he is in a good mood, he may give you a treat and perhaps chop out your appendix or some other stray part of your fine, masculine anatomy, free of charge. Dr Serein is a generous man, and a great performer with the knife; such artists are often persuaded to give encores.'

She had smeared some shaving soap above and below his knee, but her hand strayed up to his thigh, almost but not quite touching his testicles. Donald went to guide her hand, and at that moment the phone at his bedside emitted a buzz like an avenging wasp.

Maureen giggled at his anguish: he rolled his eyes in a silent supplication to an unsympathetic deity, and picked up the phone. It was Sandra.

He listened to Sandra's apology for not coming to see him, and as he informed her that he was quite comfortable, Maureen's light touch caused him to squirm in divine discomfort, while at the very moment that he assured her that he was being well treated, his playful nurse ran the shaving brush tantalizingly around and over his genitals, sending a tingling through his body. But as soon as he had put the phone down again, Maureen's attention was diverted back to the shaving in earnest of his leg. It was another five minutes before she set down the basin and shaving gear and carefully dried him with the towel. With one deft tug, she pulled off her panties and tights, kicked off her shoes, and jumped into the bed beside him.

'I dare not undress properly,' she said, 'in case anybody comes into the room, but I am sure that a great, outstanding fellow like yourself can manage to provide a lonely maiden with a fleeting pleasure. Oh,' she added, giving him a mischievous tweak, 'perhaps I should have said upstanding!'

It was the quickest of quickies. Both of them were aware of the possibility of their being disturbed, and the danger of their being discovered added a spice to their enjoyment. Donald was groping through the folds of her uniform: her breasts, when he reached them, were full and rich and as he caressed them, she demonstrated her approval by the rolling of her tongue against his and by the ardour with which she inserted his long, tormented penis. There could have been a raging furnace within her, she made love with such fiery abandon. The warmth of her body filled him with longing, but he had no time to do more than snatch at the bliss of their loving as it was offered. She drove him to a wild, explosive climax without giving him a second's respite, and she held him tightly to her until the last spasm of his ejaculation had died away.

In the afterglow, Donald felt a pang of remorse. It had been so rapid that he started to excuse himself for not having done enough for her.

'I like it when we steal a moment under the noses of the great men of the clinic,' she laughed. 'And don't you go spoiling it by becoming all regretful like some penitent sinner. It was fine for me, and as for it being all over in a flash, just you wait, my lad, until you are lying here, recuperating after your operation. You have no idea what I shall do to you then. And I might even work my will on you when you are sleeping peacefully under the anaesthetic. Every nurse is something of a necrophiliac.'

She had got her clothes back in order and had thrust her feet into her shoes. She smoothed her hair, bent over and bestowed a farewell kiss on his forehead, and had tripped out of the room before he had recovered his breath.

At about the same time that Dr Serein was examining his patient, his colleague, Dr Jean Gaveau, left the Clinique St-André and went to the Villa Rose. Although the house of pleasure was only a few hundred yards from the house of pain, he took his car, but took the precaution of parking it in a side street. Peering anxiously over his shoulder to make sure that he was not observed, and with his coat collar pulled up like a film gangster, he hurried inside.

'Your friends are waiting for you in the Lilac Room, that is number five,' the coquettish girl behind the desk told him.

He knocked, and Andrew Drummond opened the door and beckoned him inside.

Gaveau was a short, dark man of perhaps forty-five, and was on the tubby side. To look at his rather flabby hands, nobody would have taken him for the brilliant surgeon that he was, and he had a nervousness about his movements which was intensified by his present situation.

'What is all this about?' he demanded of Drummond.

'My two friends and myself require your help,' was the smooth reply, and Drummond outlined what he wanted Gaveau to do.

'You are out of your mind,' protested the Frenchman. 'It would never work, and I would be disgraced and lose my place at the Clinic. You would ruin me.'

'If I were to tell what I know about you, that would ruin you.'

'What is this guilty secret?' Anna demanded.

'That is none of your business,' Gaveau retorted hotly.

'Come now, Jean, that is no way to speak to a lady.' Drummond turned to her with a smile. 'I knew him at Medical School, and I had to extricate him from a sordid adventure that he had got himself into with a little boy, a refugee from Vietnam.'

'Is a homosexual affair such a dreadful scandal these days?' Isis asked.

'That depends,' Drummond answered. 'If you are handling the bodies of extremely wealthy patients in an ultra-conservative clinic, it could get you the sack. And there were other features of the liaison. The boy was only ten years old, and when he, egged on by his parents no doubt, tried to put the screw on poor, weak-willed Jean, he met with a very unfortunate accident.'

211

'That was your doing,' Gaveau accused. 'You castrated the child!'

'Nonsense!' Drummond was amused. 'The brat only lost one ball, but his family understood that if they persisted in their attempt to blackmail you, he would be deprived of the other, and that would really have been serious. But nobody would believe that you were not the culprit, in the light of your entanglement. Tell me, Jean, do you still fondle the buttocks of sweet, fresh little boys or have you learned your lesson?'

Gaveau shook his head impatiently. 'You would not bring this up again, not now.'

'You know very well that I would, otherwise you would not have come,' Drummond replied contemptuously. 'Now, shall we get down to details?'

But Gaveau was still reluctant, and they sensed that there was another motive as well as fear that lay behind his behaviour. Drummond was on the verge of losing his temper.

'We do not have the time to act the fool,' he snapped. 'Will you do what is necessary to get us away, or are you prepared to face exposure and scandal?'

A cunning leer came over Gaveau's face, and he turned towards Isis.

'Never mind all this talk about the past. You look a woman of character, not at all the sort of person who should find herself in trouble, and for your sake, I shall take the risk of helping all of you.'

'Good, let's go,' Drummond said.

But Gaveau's eyes were still fixed on Isis, and he showed no inclination to leave.

'It's not only young boys that I find attractive,' he confided. 'Just occasionally I come across a woman who really arouses me. Wouldn't you think it natural for me to expect from you some gesture of gratitude for the way I am imperilling my future for you?'

'You want me to make love to you?' she gasped. 'Here and now?'

'What better place?' Gaveau replied. 'And certainly now, before I have delivered. How can I be sure that, afterwards, you would not have grown cool towards me?'

Isis recoiled. But before she could pour scorn on her aspiring suitor, Drummond intervened.

'That's very fair. I suggest that the two of you get down to business on this bed. I do not think that it would be wise to leave you on your own, so the other lady and I can divert ourselves on this commodious chaise-longue.'

For Isis, it was the ultimate humiliation. She hated the greasy, plump doctor, but could not refuse his greedy fingers, and when he thrust his tongue inside her mouth, she had to fight back the wave of nausea. His cock was an unpleasant shade of purple with heavy veins which throbbed menacingly. She could not resist him, but she did nothing to enhance his pleasure. Yet her very passivity seemed to excite him. It was rape and he knew it, and it heightened his enjoyment to know that she did not want him, but had to accept whatever he inflicted on her. Her body was limp, her mouth unresponsive. The greater her loathing, the more intense was the rapture of Jean Gaveau.

Isis prayed for it to end, and turned her face away in disgust. She was looking at Drummond and Anna, locked in a passionate embrace on the chaise-longue. Anna was making tiny moans, as she arched her back to meet Andrew's sensual movements. He was not driving into Anna in the insensate way that Gaveau was violating her body, but sliding slowly, so that she could enjoy to the full every quiver of his fine, proud cock. Anna was twisting as though there was an inner fire which was consuming her but which was also her fulfilment.

'OK, give it to me, now,' she begged. 'I want every last drop, now, now, now!'

Anna's frenzy was infectious. Despite herself, Isis felt her own haunches rising and falling in time with those of Andrew Drummond. Now it was Gaveau who wanted to hold back, but she would not let him. She gripped him with savage force and pumped him mercilessly. She heard Anna scream, and she and Drummond rolled off the chaise-longue in the grip of their orgasm.

'Come, damn you!' Isis hissed viciously at Gaveau, and she stepped up the pace and the pressure.

'Wait, please!' he whimpered.

But she was implacable and her disgust was strangely tempered with delight at her reversing their roles, the raper raped. His climax was virtually a collapse, and she threw his inert body away from her as if it were a defilement.

They cleaned themselves up and dressed. Gaveau gazed at Isis resentfully, and Drummond slapped him on the back.

'Well,' he beamed, 'you have had your pound of flesh, and rather more. Let's be on our way.'

The four of them trooped out. Drummond paid for the room and Gaveau led them to his car. He hustled them inside, in dread that they would be discovered, and drove off.

Three minutes later, the three fugitives were safely lodged in a room at the Clinique St-André which was reserved for the patients of Dr Gaveau.

It was more comfortable than a cell, but Milos knew that the house was for him a prison. He sat on the divan, staring at the blank wall opposite. He had no idea of what would happen to him, and no longer cared. Sandra had been in danger, and he had saved her. That was all that mattered: a moral debt had been repaid.

The door opened, and to his amazement Sandra walked in. Her features were serious and resolute. Milos gazed at her as though he were beholding a revelation of the Kingdom of Heaven.

'I've come to thank you for saving my life,' she said.

'I love you,' he replied simply.

She kissed him tenderly, but he grasped her and thrust his tongue deep inside her mouth, as if he could explore the depths of her being. With him so close to her, she felt all the old fascination and she knew that she had always wanted him. Pulling herself free, she started to undress, without any trace of self-consciousness or coquettish flirtatiousness. Milos gazed at her, unable to believe his eyes.

'Someone might come in,' he warned her.

'Nobody will disturb us,' she assured him. 'And what if they did? I am not ashamed of you: would you get all het up at being seen with me?'

She stood before him, proud in her nakedness, and he feasted his eyes on the mouth-watering beauty of her flesh. Sandra regarded him in mild amusement.

'Aren't you going to take off your clothes?' she demanded. 'Or have you gone all bashful?'

Milos pulled himself together, and the warm smile which she had seen before so rarely flickered across his face.

'Forgive me. It's all been rather sudden. I would not be so impolite to keep my clothes on in front of a lady.'

He pulled off the offending garments, and led her to the divan. Sandra had never seen his body before: it had a solid, chunky look about it which she found appealing, and his firm, meaty penis was definitely appetizing. What she had envisaged originally as a mere 'mercy fuck' had developed into something far more promising.

Milos laid her down gently and knelt beside her. His hands touched her body, as a blind man might have attempted to learn everything about her from his fingertips. And where his fingers led, his lips followed. She closed her eyes and succumbed to her growing excitement. His mouth was at her throat, and then he was lasciviously licking her nipples, which stiffened in a silent acknowledgement of her pleasure. But when she went to go down on him, he shook his head.

'We have so little time,' he said, 'I don't want to let your face out of my sight for a second.'

So they made love, face to face, trying to cram a lifetime into the one fleeting encounter. Around his eyes were the tiny lines of care and strain, and she tried to rub them away, and to bring him a sort of inner peace even while their bodies were striving in the joyful conflict of sex. And Milos felt the icy barriers which his breakdown had created in his mind melting away before the warmth of her embrace.

'Just keep doing what you are doing,' Sandra purred.

He pressed his mouth hard against hers, and her teeth were biting his lip, her hands scratching the taut muscles of his shoulders. As he slid easily and lovingly within her, she seemed to be pulling him back, reluctant to lose the feeling of him for a moment. She could sense the onset of his climax, and although she wanted it to go on and on, she knew that it had to be a once only deal, and her quivering eagerness told him that she was ready to come with him. His thrusts grew more compelling and she clung to him even more tightly; they were fighting for breath and the last vestige of control vanished before the marvellous onrush to the wild abandon of their orgasm. Again and again his penis erupted, while her vagina was pulsating as if it were dancing for delight.

'That was cosmic,' Sandra breathed, when they finally sorted out their intertwined limbs.

Milos could not remember the last time he had felt so perfectly relaxed and in harmony with the world. The weeks and months which had separated them fell away. The present, that instant of sheer wonder, annihilated time. He stroked her hair and wished that life was a simpler matter and that they could stay together always. Still, if they had to say goodbye, there could not be a nicer way of doing so. Sandra seemed to be aware of what was going on in his mind, and tried to cover any regrets over their ephemeral affair with a flippancy she did not feel.

'So, tell me, my great macho warrior, isn't fucking better than fighting?' she teased.

'A fucking sight better,' he agreed.

'And who needs a Golden Phallus?' she asked.

'Nobody, but you can be sure that people will go on fighting for it,' Milos answered mockingly.

There was a knock on the door, and a voice called, 'Monsieur Milos, your lunch is ready.'

'Just a moment,' Milos answered, as they scrambled into their clothes. 'Do you know,' he said to Sandra, 'that meal has given me quite an appetite.'

They kissed goodbye, and as she turned to go, Sandra saw that there were tears in Milos's eyes, and yet he was also smiling. She walked out of the room, and out of his life, and she realized that her cheeks also were wet.

'So where do we go from here? Back to Salamba?'

Isis put the question to Drummond, but he shook his head.

'We cannot be sure that Milos will not get away, and if

he does he will be ready to murder us because of the way you treated his beloved Sandra. In fact, you had better get a message as soon as we are out of here to Grunwald to move the rest of the sect out of the country, and to take with them the statue of Osiris. He can swing that; his bank is always moving huge consignments of gold. We can write off the dream of the temple in Ibari.'

They were interrupted by the arrival of Gaveau. He scowled at them.

'Well, it took one hell of a lot of fixing, but the plane will be ready in the morning. You understand that from the minute that you leave here, my responsibility for you is over. Do you know where you are going?'

'We were on the point of deciding when you came in,' Drummond told him.

Suddenly Anna spoke.

'We fly to Rome.' There was a determination in her voice which carried conviction. 'I have a house there, and now that Moriba is dead, it is not known to anybody.'

'Why should we simply fall in with whatever suits you?' Isis demanded angrily.

'Because I am the only living person who knows where the Golden Head of Osiris is hidden. So you will do as I say.'

Andrew Drummond did not say anything, but looking at him, Isis knew that she was no longer their leader.

The following day was an eventful one. It started early for Donald McFee, on the operating table, under the nimble, skilful hands of Dr Serein. He was unconscious when an ambulance drove out of the Clinique St-André to the private airfield at Le Bourget. There was the minimum of fuss since the patient in the ambulance was in a coma, and her doctor and nurse were getting her to the surgery of a Dr Cavallieri without delay. There was a letter of authorization signed by a well-known Paris surgeon, Dr Gaveau, and although the emigration officers did not know it, he too had obtained the passports for all three passengers.

As the plane soared away from Paris, Andrew Drummond relaxed for the first time since the affray in the Rue Achille. In her nurse's uniform, Anna looked unusually demure, and really rather dishy, he judged. Isis, on the other hand, exhibited a deathly pallor. She was sleeping as soundly as Donald, but she would not be awake again until long after she had landed and, with her attendant doctor and nurse, been rushed somewhere in Rome, far from the surgery of Dr Cavallieri, if he existed.

It was in the afternoon that Milos had another visitor. The man did not identify himself, but he spoke with great authority.

'President Milos, you have placed our administration in an embarrassing position. The Republic of France believes in the rule of law and the punishment of crimes. However, we have to take notice of the fact that the man you killed was as undesirable a scoundrel as has ever walked the earth. Trying you before a French court would arouse a lot of unpleasant publicity both in your country and in our own. We have decided therefore that the murderer was a Herr Brodsky, who has for the moment escaped. You, President Milos, were in Vienna at the time of the incident. You understand, sir, you have never been here.'

The man stared hard at Milos to make sure that this strangely deranged ruler of a sovereign state did understand.

'A plane is waiting for you at Charles de Gaulle and will take you to Vienna. I suggest that you return to your own country from there openly. And now, Mr President, if you are ready, shall we be going?'

# 14
## Dragon's Teeth

'Welcome home, Mr President,' said Asombolo. 'I hope that your trip has been worthwhile.'

'I feel a lot better,' replied Milos. 'My medical advisers administered a kind of shock treatment. It did not take long, but it certainly was severe.'

'I did not expect you back so soon.'

'I wanted to return to Salamba in time for the next attempted revolution,' explained Milos with heavy irony.

'You should not have hurried,' grinned Asombolo, 'you would have received an invitation. Now, do you need a period of convalescence?'

'No, I am quite my old self again. Let's get down to business.'

Asombolo reported to Milos on what had occurred in Salamba during his absence.

'Oh yes, and a funny thing happened yesterday morning,' he concluded. 'Those friends of yours, the ones who were going to establish some sort of temple here, simply packed up their things and cleared out, without a word of warning.'

'Did they now,' Milos mused, 'and did they by any chance remove that big golden statue which they had erected in their temple?'

'Yes, of course,' Asombolo answered. 'The Swiss guy, Grunwald, told me the day before they left that it was some sort of cult object, very old but of no monetary value. It was not gold, you know, only painted.'

'He told you that, did he?'

Milos did not bother to press Asombolo for an answer.

He was not surprised to learn later that on the day that Isis's birds had flown, Grunwald's bank had arranged a shipment of bullion out of Ibari. On this same flight, there had been a number of crates which purported to contain 'miscellaneous objects of archaeological interest'. They had not been examined by customs officials.

Milos wondered how much Asombolo had received in a Swiss bank account for turning a blind eye, and for allowing himself to be convinced that all that glisters is not gold.

A week after the raid in the Rue Achille, the mysterious assailants had not been caught. The police appeared to be taking a very relaxed view; the press soon found other more sensational events to report, and public interest evaporated.

Professor Louis Halevy went about his daily routine as if nothing out of the ordinary had happened, but in view of the rout of the forces of Isis, he did remove one irksome restriction. As the university term drew to its close, Petra left the students' hostel and moved in with him.

It was a Sunday morning, and the couple were enjoying lying in bed late. They had made love, then Halevy had gone into the kitchen and made breakfast, which they had eaten in bed. Then they had made love again, and now were talking about getting up.

'Donald is being discharged from the clinic this morning,' Halevy said. 'We must be out of bed by the time he and Sandra come round.'

'Why?' Petra asked. 'You know what a horny couple they are; we shall only have to get back in again.'

'You may be right,' Halevy conceded.

They made love.

It was an hour later when the taxi drew up, and Sandra

and Donald emerged. His leg was heavily bandaged, and he walked with a limp, but he had been told that, provided he kept out of fights for the next month, his knee should heal satisfactorily and he might be fit enough to resume his career.

'We must celebrate before you go back to London, although I am sure that we have not heard the last of the Isis gang,' Halevy told them. 'They have gone to earth, but they will sprout up again some time, as dangerous as ever. But tonight, we shall have company. Professor Khalid is arriving from Cairo to take delivery at last of the Golden Phallus.'

'It will be strange, not having it around the place,' Petra said. 'I think that we should profit from having it here one more time.'

'We don't need a lump of old metal, do we, Sandy!' Donald kissed Sandra affectionately, and fondled her breast. 'You are the one woman I love, and that is all that counts.'

As he spoke, in his mind's eye, he conjured up the image of Maureen, snuggling up to him behind the screens around his bed, and he smelt once more the nurse's very special odour, sexy and sanitary.

Sandra kissed him with a passion that she had not experienced since that highly charged session with Milos.

'I adore you,' she murmured to Donald. Then, turning to Halevy, 'Why don't we take your friend, Khalid, to The Double Cross tonight?'